FORCED AFFECTION

Jeanne squalled, "Get over there, you. With him."

Regan said, "Do as she says, Sara. Quickly."

Sara obeyed. Regan got up beside her, gripped her arm.

"This is better, much better," Jeanne said. She waved menacingly. "Kiss her."

"What?"

"You heard me. Kiss her."

He looked at Sara's face, saw the way her chin was quivering. He kissed her lightly on the cheek.

"You call that a kiss? Put your arms around her, hold her." Jeanne laughed hysterically. "Kiss her. I want those mouths open, those tongues working!"

He tried.

"Good. Pretty good," Jeanne said. "Now strip down."

Sara was already pulling off her sweater. He looked at her and saw a glint in her eyes, a curious expression he had never seen before . . .

Love
Fever

Jay Carr

WILDSIDE PRESS

1

DR. PAUL REGAN rose and stretched his arms high, arching his back, fighting the depression he always experienced after a session with Sheila Michaels. The girl suffered from a deep melancholia. Slowly, ploddingly, painstakingly, step by cautious step, she was rising from the depths with his professional help— yet he always felt this depression after she left.

Today's session with her had been good, one of the best during the four months she had been consulting him. There had been little of the usual self-castigation and self-criticism. She had accepted his casual compliment about the new way she was wearing her hair, had even primped a trifle, smiling, allowing herself the luxury of the tiniest flirtation with him. She had gone so far as to tell him about the new man in the apartment on her floor who had asked her to dinner. Frank? Fred? Something like that. He would have to check it on the tape, and casually bring up the name some time in the future.

Yes, Paul told himself, it had been a good session. Soon, with his help, Sheila would rejoin the great mass of humanity that managed to exist with a certain degree of adjustment, even happiness. She would find herself a man to replace the one she had lost. She would fill the emotional void within her. And he would have accomplished, at least with her, what he had set out to do so long ago.

Then why this depression?

He shrugged. There was still Jeanne with her erotic obsession and Robert with his neurasthenia and Helen with her anxiety neurosis. And of course, his own wife, Grace, with her morbid jealousy.

Paul felt a throbbing pain at the base of his neck, and his stomach was protesting its lack of a proper lunch, and he had another intake interview to get through this afternoon—and he suddenly remembered that Grace had made bridge plans for the evening, and . . .

He smiled to himself: maybe he needed a psychiatrist. The cornball jest amused him, and he laughed aloud. His guffaws bounced back at him from the walls of the office. He turned and walked to the wide windows overlooking the street.

The noise and confusion of the late afternoon reached up to him; but he was safe, above it all, in this secluded room, alone and yet not alone, the problems of so many others always within him.

Here in California, in this resort and aircraft community of Beach City, some eighty miles north of Los Angeles, the great sun god beckoned to him, laughed at him in his safety. It was mid-October, and Paul could remember the crisp fall air, the promise of snow back in his native Illinois. But here the sun was still warm and demanding. He could visualize the people below, the women in tight-fitting shorts and Capri pants, flaunting their femininity, and the men in their sweaty suits, hurrying and scurrying, each one a prospective patient. How many would find their way to Dr. Paul Regan? The thought was strangely uncomfortable, and a faint wave of nausea swept through him.

He made a mental note: from now on, no matter what, he would take a full hour at lunch, go somewhere and eat in relaxed fashion.

Regan, at thirty-eight, still had the build of the athlete he had been in his younger days—wide of shoulder, narrow of hip, flat in the stomach. His hair was dark and unruly, his face deeply tanned, with a strong nose and dark, sympathetic eyes, wide mouth. There was a scar an inch long under his left cheekbone, light against the tan. He wore brown flannel slacks, chocolate-colored sports jacket, tan shirt, knitted tie.

He had been in Beach City three years now, had made a place for himself through his successful psychiatric practice and his twice-weekly lectures at the University, as well as through marriage to a local girl—a member of one of the oldest and most respected families in Beach City. And in Beach City, such things counted. Having worked long years to reach his present position, Paul was happy and contented; or so he had been telling himself more and more often of late.

The door opened. "I'm sorry, Dr. Regan. I didn't mean to intrude."

He sighed without turning. "That's all right, Sara."

"There's still Miss Hopkins this afternoon."

7

"Yes. Has she come in yet?"

"I don't think so. I didn't see her go by."

His offices consisted of this large consultation room, tastefully and expensively furnished, a smaller reception room leading to the hallway of the third floor of the building (the Winston Building, named after his wife's paternal grandfather), plus a third room, the smallest, which opened into the consultation room and also had a door to the hallway. The small room was his private study and retreat; it was always cluttered the way he liked it.

"Dr. Regan," Sara said hesitantly. "I—"

He turned. Sara Richter was twenty-three, petite, twittery as a canary at times, proud of her unexpectedly large breasts, as was obvious from her choice of clothes. She had big, brown eyes and a sensitive face, and should not have been wasting her nights alone in movie theaters, as Regan knew she did. He was writing a book on fanatic personalities, compiling it from a series of lectures he was giving at the University, and he had hired Sara out of the University typing pool to help him with the book. She was intelligent, a willing worker, a former psychology major; he had found her helpful. In the beginning, they had worked only at night and then, somehow or other, she was coming in during the day, invading his study, arranging his appointments, doing more and more of his clerical work. She could see the hallway from her desk.

He was thankful for one facet of her personality —she had never tried to tidy up that little room.

She still stood uncertainly before him, hesitating to voice what was on her mind.

8

"What is it, Sara?"

She licked her lips. "I know how you feel after seeing Mrs. Michaels."

"Do you?"

"I think so."

"And?"

"And," she said, with a shrug.

"Thanks for the thought," he said.

"You are entirely welcome," she said primly.

"Sara, I know you mean well, and I'm not going to lecture you about professional ethics. You know by now that I never discuss any of my patients or my reactions to them. I appreciate your concern. Need I say more?"

"No."

"You're a good . . ." he began.

"Never mind, doctor. It's almost four-thirty, and Miss Hopkins should be coming along soon."

"They're usually late for the first appointment."

She smiled. "I thought you didn't discuss patients."

He laughed. "You win, Sara."

She turned to his desk, idly, straightened his notebook and pen. "I feel sorry for her," she said.

"You don't even know Mrs. Michaels. You know nothing about her."

"That doesn't change the situation," she said.

"Sara," he said, "I'm afraid you feel sorry for everyone who comes in here."

"Perhaps."

"Even me?" asked a new voice.

Regan turned, startled. He hadn't heard the reception room door opening. His wife stood there, smiling self-consciously, as if aware that she had interrupted

9

something. She was quite aware, also, of how he felt about her coming to the office; yet here she was.

Sara's hand flew to her mouth. "Why, good afternoon, Mrs. Regan."

"Hello, Sara. Are you taking good care of my husband?"

"Grace," interrupted Paul, "you know—"

"If you'll excuse me, Dr. Regan," Sara said.

He forced back the sudden anger at his wife. "Of course, Sara. You can go on home."

Sara retreated into the small room, giving him a sympathetic smile, and closed the door behind her. He waited a moment before crossing to the other door and glancing into the reception room. Miss Hopkins had not yet arrived. He was thankful for that, at least.

Turning, closing the door behind him, he saw that Grace had seated herself on the couch. She was staring at the painting on the opposite wall, as if seeing it for the first time—as if something in it fascinated her.

Paul walked up to her. "Grace, why did you come here? I've asked you to stay away from the office."

"And I know why," she said, not looking at him. "Identification with the analyst and all that crap. How about me identifying with my husband for a change?"

Grace was tall and elegant and well-bred, one of the most beautiful women Paul had ever seen, a fact which in his opinion had a lot to do with her troubles. Her hair was soft and reddish-brown, worn in loose waves that were the envy of other women; her expressive oval face was molded in the classic lines, almost too perfect in its symmetry, with deep blue

10

eyes that had the habit of focusing on one object for a long time, as if trying to memorize its every small detail. She was a product of the best private schools, and her occasional usage of language such as *crap* and certain other pungent words was her method of trying to shock people.

"Please, Grace," he said, "let's not quarrel."

"She has the largest bazooms for a woman her size!"

"What? Who are you talking about?"

"They are much larger than mine, and she must be at least six inches shorter than I."

"Grace, this kind of talk is absurd. I have a patient due here."

"A woman, no doubt." She frowned, as if deep in thought. "I agree with you, Paul. We must be adult and clinical and all that kind of horse manure. It's just that my husband happens to be a psychiatrist and he happens to have half the attractive women in this town telling him all their sexual problems, how cold and misunderstanding their husbands are and how twin beds are not conducive to loving." She grinned, slowly removing a pumpkin-colored glove from her left hand, slapping the glove against her thigh. "Her bazooms are large, you know."

"Yes, I know. I have noticed."

"And she is in love with you."

"Grace—"

"Are you going to analyze me now, dear? Please don't. I know what I am. I'm jealous and I'm not hiding it."

"Will you please leave?"

She patted the couch, almost lovingly. "A little

11

narrow," she said, "but I suppose it serves the purpose. Much better than the back seat of a car, I'll say that. Do they give you all the details, Paul, all the intimate and tiny little details? You must have a difficult time. It must be something like reading the same pornographic book over and over again, or keeping a collection of dirty pictures. Is it like that, darling?"

"You know better."

She laughed and stood up, breathing deeply, staring at him. "Now you are appealing to my intelligence. You're clever, Dr. Paul Regan and I—and I—" She turned her head away from him and he could see the tears welling up in her eyes. A sob racked her body. "And I'm a damned fool." She turned back to him, smiling bravely, wiping the back of a hand across her eyes. "I'm jealous, period, end of statement."

"You knew what it would be like."

"Yes, Paul. I knew. You told me all about it."

He crossed to her, took her in his arms. He held her tenderly, listening to her breathing. After a moment or so, she lifted her head, looked up into his face, smiling. She planted a gentle kiss on his cheek, and then her mouth moved quickly over his, her tongue searching, and he felt her body writhe against his, demanding, wanting. He pushed her away.

"You promise so much," he said bitterly, watching her poke at her hair. She took a compact from her purse, did something quickly and efficiently to her lips.

"There's more than a promise there," she said.

"Grace, I love you."

She nodded. "You say it so well, darling."

"I mean it."

"I know you do."

"You must realize, about—"

"Oh, Paul, I do. I do! I've read all the right books and I've listened to you and, after all, I'm not un-intelligent or all wrapped up in various neuroses." She placed a hand on his arm. "It's been a bitch of a day, darling. Put it down to that. Everything seemed to go wrong. I played golf at the club this morning. I was eleven over par and that silly little Hendersen woman beat me. I'm sure she cheated."

"Charlotte Hendersen?"

"Yes, darling. What other Hendersen woman?"

So that was it; that had set her off. He could understand it better now. He should have known it was something like this. Charlotte Hendersen had been a patient of his for more than a year; she had gone through an incomplete analysis with him and then he had advised her to go elsewhere for therapy. There had been too much identification with Paul.

"My work is something you'll have to learn to live with, Grace."

"I know, I know. She's such a bitch, Paul. I could scratch her eyes out and, frankly, it would give me the greatest of pleasure to see her tortured. She always gives me that look, that damned knowing look, as if to say how much more she knows than I do, how much more you and she have shared. . . . Paul, I'm sorry. I'm acting like a child, a spoiled child at that."

There were so many things Paul wanted to say to

her, but he had said them all before, and there was no time now.

He could remember his own psychoanalysis with Dr. Bemelman. The good and kindly man had advised him, above everything else, to be careful about the eventual choice of a wife. "She will have to be a remarkable person, Paul," he had said. "She will have to be all things to you, a woman who can understand your needs and desires, a woman able to push aside nagging doubts about what you do, why and how you do it. You know, Paul, in our society, for the great mass of the people, psychoanalysis and sex are almost synonymous. That's an unfortunate fact in our life."

And Paul had been careful in his choice, to be sure. Grace had been all he wanted, beautiful and intelligent, and . . . He smiled; his thoughts were drifting. He certainly didn't need to convince himself of his love for Grace.

She grinned at him. "Darling, you won't be late? We're playing bridge with Mike and Doris."

"I know."

"My apologies, Paul. Will you accept them?"

"In the middle of the night, in the darkness, when there is nothing but the beauty that is you and the desire that is me . . . I'll tell you what you can do with your apologies."

She laughed. "You're insane."

"Naturally." He enjoyed the sound of her laughter; it was free and easy and natural. "And now, dear little wife, will you please get your dear little can out of my office so that I can get back to work?"

"You're hard-hearted, Dr. Paul Regan." She turned,

14

looking at the painting again. It was a mélange of softly subdued colors, blending together to give a strange feeling of tranquility.

"I don't like that," she said, and her tone was serious.

"You gave it to me."

"I know I did."

"Get going."

"Yes, boss," she said. "Anything you say. But I still don't like that painting."

"We'll burn it," he said, jokingly.

"Promise me?" She was staring at him intently.

"I promise you," he said, without thinking.

"Let's make it a big production, voodoo and all that. I'll stick needles in it and we'll build a little platform in the back yard and—"

"We'll do that. Later."

"All right, all right. I can take a hint."

His easy humor with her was on the surface only. Inside, he was concerned, and he was wondering how much longer this would go on. They had been married just over a year, and these indications of pathological jealousy had been growing over the past few months. The painting, titled *Peace*, had been a gift from Grace to celebrate their first month of marriage. He liked it, enjoyed it—and now, as he thought about it, he remembered that it had been painted by a local artist, a woman named Sandy Mannings. He also remembered that it had been only last week that he had met Sandy Mannings. Grace had introduced her. And now she was thinking of sticking needles into the painting, burning it. . . .

He walked to the door with her, opened it for her.

He saw the woman sitting in the reception room, leafing through a magazine. The woman looked up and saw them at the same time.

Grace smiled, needlessly, said in a too-loud voice, "Until later, darling," and walked out of the office.

The woman said, "She's quite beautiful."

"Yes."

"I suppose . . . even the beautiful ones have their problems."

"I imagine."

"Do your patients usually call you *darling?*"

"As it happens, that was my wife."

The woman smiled. "Oh? Well, she's beautiful anyhow. And I happen to be Jessica Hopkins, and I've been waiting."

"Of course," Regan said. "I'm sorry for the delay."

2

An intake interview was so important and yet, as Paul followed Jessica Hopkins into the other room, his mind was wandering. He could not forget Grace's fits of jealousy. He was wondering just how and when he would be able to bring the subject up with her. Certainly not tonight, not with Mike and Doris coming for bridge. During the weekend, perhaps? He had to get at the crux of her jealousy, let her see for herself how ridiculous it was.

"I can come back at another time, if it's more convenient."

"What?"

"You *are* Dr. Regan, aren't you?"

"My apologies, Miss Hopkins. Really, there is no excuse for my poor manners."

"Your manners don't seem too professional, doctor." She grinned away the insult in her words. "But I would suppose that even an analyst must have his personal problems."

"You would suppose correctly, Miss Hopkins."

17

"Shall I analyze you, or should we have it the usual way?"

He laughed, motioning to the soft leather chair next to his desk. She was tall, almost as tall as Grace, with intensely black hair cut in no particular style, as if she were merely acknowledging that it was there and she had to do something about it. Yet the careless tresses were attractive, and so was she. Her complexion was clear, slightly tanned, marked by a thin line of freckles running beneath her eyes and across the bridge of her nose. The mouth was wide, the lips full, and the only makeup she wore was a hint of lipstick. Her teeth, when she smiled at him, were large and startlingly white. But it was her eyes that held his interest. They were a clear, curious tint of bluish-green; and they were interested eyes, eyes that saw and understood much. Paul sensed a troubled sadness, too, in those eyes. She had high, full breasts, and Paul found himself wondering if Grace had noted this; probably yes, and she would make some comment later about the big bazooms.

Miss Hopkins was dressed in a frost-blue suit with a pleated skirt and a short jacket. Her high-heeled pumps and handbag were a matching darker blue. Her only jewelry was a charm bracelet on her left wrist.

She sat down, opened the bag, took out cigarettes and matches, closed the purse again. She silently offered him a cigarette, and he shook his head, indicating the brass pipe rack and humidor on the desk.

"A sign of strength," she said, "and of judgment and perseverance."

"What?" He held a match for her cigarette.

"The pipes. Aren't they there to indicate your character?"

He pushed an ashtray across the desk then took a briar from the rack, fondling it gently, and sat down in his swivel chair.

"I'm afraid not, Miss Hopkins. They are there only for my own pleasure."

"Was it Freud who said that all smoking is only a symptom of frustration? Aren't pipes and cigarettes and cigars all phallic symbols?"

"Are they? I don't know."

"Are you a Freudian or a Jungian, Dr. Regan?"

"Does it matter to you?"

"Not really."

"I didn't think so, Miss Hopkins."

She looked around the room, her glance finally settling on the painting. "I like that," she said. "I like that very much."

He slowly filled his pipe from the humidor, watching her at the same time. She showed only a few signs of nervousness in his presence: the way she had crossed her legs, too carefully, the way one foot swung back and forth. He had the feeling that she would usually expect to be in control of any situation in which she found herself; she would be, to her way of thinking at any rate, self-sufficient, undemanding of others.

He let the silence lengthen while he lit his pipe, blowing clouds of smoke towards the ceiling. The room was quiet and comfortable now, with Grace gone. His depression had disappeared.

"Harold Stern suggested that I consult you."

"I know. How is he? I haven't seen Harold in some time."

"He's overworked and understaffed. He'll drop dead of a heart attack one of these days, and only a few of us will realize how much good he has done for Beach City." She shook her head. "I should correct that: how much good he has tried to do for Beach City."

"He's a dedicated man."

Harold Stern had resigned his professorship at the University to head a local welfare group. Paul knew him only slightly, but he knew that Jessica Hopkins was connected in some way with Stern's group.

"I suppose," she said, tamping out her cigarette in the ashtray, "I should tell you something about myself."

"Only if you feel like it."

She laughed. "The intake interview," she said, still laughing. "Let the patient feel completely at ease. Listen with your quote, third ear, unquote; let the patient do the talking. Oh, Dr. Regan, I know the story."

"You seem to be an intelligent young woman."

"I am. I freely admit it. Why shouldn't I? My IQ, according to Stanford-Binet, is one hundred and fifty-two, and I hold a master's degree in child psychology." She leaned forward slightly, staring into his face, and he could see the way her breasts swung slightly with the movement; he was suddenly positive she wasn't wearing a brassiere. "I am most intelligent, Dr. Regan. I have read Freud and Jung and I think Dr. Schweitzer is the greatest man in the world, and I know all the terminology you're going to throw at me, if I give you the chance. I understand a great many things."

"Undoubtedly you do," he said, quietly. "Your general knowledge probably is very high. You've probably read a great deal and it's obvious that your interests are varied." He paused. "Possibly the only thing you don't understand, or at least one of the few things, is yourself."

"Touché," she said.

"And that is why you are here."

"And that is why I am here."

"And?"

"And nothing, Dr. Regan."

"All right," he said.

He leaned back in the swivel chair, relaxed, unassuming. Dimly, somewhere deep in his psyche, something his grandmother had told him flitted across, was gone, and he reached for it and couldn't find it. He had been orphaned at the age of eight, raised by his maternal grandmother. . . .

"Where did you get that scar?" she asked.

"The war."

"How romantic."

"War is not romantic, Miss Hopkins."

"I suppose not. But not having gone through one, I couldn't really say. I have been to Europe, traveled extensively, and I have seen the destruction. I wonder why we try to destroy each other in such inane ways, Dr. Regan. I read a story or a book once; I can't remember the title. But the people in it were so civilized, so knowing. They simply chose by lottery, each year, a certain of their number to die, and then stoned them to death. That seems a much more civilized way to do it, don't you think?"

He shook his head, not answering.

"That's right," she went on. "You're very good at this, doctor, and I can't understand why. You have me talking and talking and I had told myself that I wasn't going to talk, that I would simply come in here as a favor to Harold Stern, smile sweetly at you, look at you, and walk out. I understand most of your patients are women and—you have quite a reputation, in case you don't know it. The good Dr. Paul Regan."

"My reputation is my concern, Miss Hopkins."

She smiled, putting another cigarette in her mouth. This time, he made no move to light it for her. "I imagine," she said, "that it is also the concern of your wife."

She was consciously trying to irritate him, make him angry—he realized that, and yet he did feel anger at the imputation about his wife and his women patients. Perhaps Grace's jealousy was becoming a matter of common gossip.

She put both hands beneath her breasts, pushed them up, fondled them, smiling at him. "I'm twenty-five years old, Dr. Regan."

"Good for you."

"How old are you?"

"Thirty-eight, if it matters."

"When I was fifteen, you were twenty-eight. How many women had you had by then?"

"Enough to satisfy me."

She smiled. "That's a good answer. I'm not a virgin."

"Not many women are, at your age."

"You would know about such things."

"I would."

"How many virgins have you—"

"That would be none of your business!"

"I guess not."

Again, there was silence between them. She was being deliberately hostile, and he wanted to let her get it out of her system.

"I've never been married," she said, after a time. "I have never wanted to be married." She leaned forward, again tamping her cigarette out in the ashtray. There was a noticeable difference this time—her hand moved jerkily, angrily, and when she looked up at him he could read the anger in her eyes. "How old were you when you married, Dr. Regan?"

"I've been married a little more than a year."

"How old was your wife when she married you?"

"Miss Hopkins," he said, smiling, "that's something you would have to ask her."

"Why?"

"You must know how women are about their ages."

"Stupid vanity," she said.

"Perhaps. Perhaps not."

"Was she a virgin?"

He turned away from her, glancing at the pale blue walls. His eyes were tired, and he still felt that ache at the base of his neck; he was still hungry. Right then, at that moment, he would have given a lot for a dry martini and the soft sound of music and a world without frustrations. . . .

"Sex seems such a disgusting and demanding part of our lives, Dr. Regan."

"Sex is what we make of it, Miss Hopkins. It can be disgusting and it can also be demanding. But it is a part of us, and we have to learn to live with it. It is something that has been with us for a good many years and probably will be with us for a good many more years."

"Do you find it disgusting?"

"No."

"Demanding?"

He laughed. "It depends whose side you're on."

She let that go. "Do you know what I do for Mr. Stern?"

"Not exactly."

"I'm a social worker, a welfare worker, call it what you want. I'm a busybody; I poke my nose in where it's not wanted. I pry and I dig and I see and I hear and I get disgusted."

"Perhaps you should change jobs."

"That would be running away, wouldn't it?"

"Is that so horrible? You sound like one of those western heroes on television."

"Let's keep my sex straight," she said, giggling. And then: "I've run away before, from other things." She rose suddenly, walked in front of the desk. "I am sorry, Dr. Regan. I am talking too much and I didn't want to talk so much. What concerns me is none of your damned business, just as whether or not your wife was a virgin when she married you is none of my damned business. I apologize for that. It was low and nasty."

"I agree."

"Thank you." She almost whispered the words.

"What other things have you run from?"

24

"They wouldn't interest you."

"Try me," said Regan. "That's what I'm here for."

"Is it? I wonder."

She turned once more, again staring at the painting on the wall. "That's so . . . I can't think of an adequate word to describe it."

"The artist called it *Peace*."

"Yes."

He was thinking of what Grace had planned to do to the painting, of the easy promise he had made to her. How could he have done that? It was a thing of beauty, almost alive, transcending its stillness . . . No, he could not destroy it. He would have to break his promise.

"Miss Hopkins," he said, "would you like to have that painting?"

She turned, slowly, looking at him, the anger and hostility gone from her eyes. Her lower lip quivered, and she shook her head.

"I mean it," he said.

"I know," she said.

"It's yours."

"No. I couldn't."

"I was going to—destroy it."

"I don't believe you."

"Please, Miss Hopkins. As a favor. Take it."

She suddenly crumpled, falling, supporting herself against the edge of the desk. He stood up quickly and went around to her. Holding her, he could feel the softness of her breasts. She would not look at him, but turned her head away. She was crying freely, and he let her go on crying; he was thinking how Grace had cried in this same room a short time

25

ago. There was a difference in the way the two women cried. Grace's tears had been demanding of recognition, sympathy, love; but this woman cried for herself, by herself, without wanting anything from him.

Good God, he thought to himself, I'm comparing this woman, this stranger, with my wife, with the woman I love. He moved away from her angrily, and crossed to the windows. It was dark now. There were the moving lights down there, the people and the machines, the frustrators and the frustrated, and the great sun god had gone for another day . . . and tomorrow would be like today and the day before and the day after . . . and then what?

He heard her moving around, the quietness of her movements on the thick carpeting. He turned in time to see her removing the painting from the wall. She was like a small child caught with its hand in the cookie jar.

"Can you manage it?" he asked. The painting was three by four feet, awkward for her.

"Yes."

They stood that way, silently watching each other, silently aware of each other.

"I've behaved very stupidly," she said.

"Not at all."

"I've been working too hard. I sometimes get emotionally involved with some of—of the people. I've been working in the Mexican section. A boy—his name was Carlos and he was coming along; he was only thirteen—he was knifed to death last week in a gang fight. I don't know, Dr. Regan. It all seemed so—so trifling and meaningless. Carlos was a good boy; his intentions were good . . . and now he is dead, and

I lie awake at night and think about him, and about all the others."

After a while he said, "You have chosen a difficult career, Miss Hopkins."

"You're most kind, Dr. Regan. I appreciate this—" she looked at the picture "—and I appreciate your letting me . . . behave the way I have. But now . . . now I have to go back into the real world."

"Will you be back?"

"I don't think so."

"I wish you would come back. I think I can help you."

"The thought is nice, really. The thought is wonderful. I'd love to come here and unburden myself to you. But—no."

"The door will always be open."

She looked at him once more, and then turned and left him alone.

The room was quiet. Nothing stirred. He stood there, feeling nothing, wanting nothing . . . and then he knew that there would be bridge tonight and, later, there would be Grace and her jealousies.

And tomorrow would be the same.

3

He enjoyed the lonely drive home each night, the chance to be completely alone, to put away the cares of the day, simply to sit comfortably behind the wheel and let his mind drift along not thinking about any of the many problems that were his responsibility. The ride was comforting, and he looked forward to it; it was almost as if, each night, he were being propelled by some external force, driving him from the world of his office, the world of mental distortions, into the world of his own existence, the world he had chosen with Grace.

But tonight was different. Tonight he felt an uneasiness, a haunting fear, as if something were happening to him that he could not even begin to understand. His two worlds were coming together, intertwining themselves, forcing themselves into each other. He had to do something about it.

His had always been a carefully controlled life, pointed toward a single goal: success. His grandmother had drilled that into him. "Whatever you set out to do, Paul," she had told him over and over, "do it well; do it as well as you can. Whether it's playing football or studying mathematics, no matter what, give it your best." And he always had given it his best, and he always had done well; there had never been any doubt about Paul Regan's success, regardless of what it was that he was after.

He had waited for his marriage, possibly because of the stress of his life, possibly because marriage, as such, had little meaning to him, possibly because of Dr. Bemelman's advice. There had been the war and the period of adjustment afterward; medical school, the years of work, of striving to make himself what he was today. Whatever his motive, he had known that he would eventually marry. In his position, marriage was almost mandatory.

There had been many women in his life. His sexual life had begun at the age of fifteen; he thoroughly and contentedly enjoyed sex, made no bones about it, although it was not an overpowering, all-consuming thing with him, as it could be with some men. The opportunities had always been there, and he had not neglected them. But there had been only two women, of the many he had known before Grace, that he had considered marrying. One had been Maria. He had traveled in Europe for a year after the war, and he had met Maria in Madrid. She was the sister of a famous bullfighter, a woman completely in love with life. Their affair had been one long battle between the sexes, a battle for survival. He had been twenty-four at the time, young and seeking and a little foolish, and there had been a moment once when he and Maria had gone to Barcelona that he had thought of asking her to marry him. But the continual war between them had helped him, in a strange way, to see himself, see the way his life was drifting, and he had returned to the United States and, eventually, to medical school. He often thought of Maria, of what his life would have been with her as his wife; he could picture her now, with that great mass of black hair, the epitome of the passionate Latin woman, entertaining his friends in Beach City. The lineup for the bedroom would have extended for blocks.

The second had been Pamela, good and sweet and kind and gentle—the girl next door, the great American dream. Pamela, for whom he had been the first man; and that had caused him great shock and consternation at the time. There had been the long, long nights, cramming his mind full of the textbooks, the coffee always there for him, her quietness and her support always there for him too—and, when he needed it, her body as well. Pamela. She had expected him to marry her—it was one of the few things in his life about which he had guilt feelings. She had wanted marriage from him, had even asked for it, and yet he could not give it to her. He had gone over his relationship with Pamela at great length with Dr. Bemelman. "Every man needs at least one woman in his life like your Pamela," Dr. Bemelman had told him. Words—thoughtful and logical words— and yet they could not possibly make up the hurt that he had inflicted on her. Occasionally, even now, he thought of her, wondered about her. He had heard she was married. . . .

Grace had been more of a find than he reasonably should have expected, and he realized it. She was

Beach City's ultimate in womanhood, wealthy, intelligent, beautiful; and he knew that she would have been the same wherever circumstances had placed her in this world. She was an orphan like himself—her father killed in the war, her mother in an auto accident.

Driving along in the quiet night, Regan could remember their first meeting.

It had been one of those dull cocktail parties. He remembered the sound of clinking glasses, the low murmur of voices, soft music somewhere in the background. He was standing with a martini in his hand, wishing he were somewhere else. He turned to see her across the room, part of a group and yet distinct from it. Her head went back slightly when she laughed. No one introduced them. They met minutes later; she gave him her cool hand, saying, "There's a horrible popular song about people like us, looking at each other across the room. I'm Grace Winston, and I've been wanting to meet you for months, Dr. Regan. I've been hearing so many nasty things about you that I can't believe they're all true."

"Unfortunately," he said, "I'm afraid most of those nasty things are true. I'm a nasty sort of guy."

That was the simple beginning. They went on from there, and Regan found himself in love, for the first time in his life, It was a strange thing to him, almost an alien emotion—he found himself in the middle of it, and it was too late to back out. . . .

Now, as he turned into his driveway, he was remembering the way it had been with Grace, the complete happiness between them. . . . Why could it not be that way again? They were both intelligent

31

people. If they could only sit down and talk this thing out, everything would be all right.

Their home was low and rambling, designed for its background of rolling hills, cypress trees, and the ocean. Building it had been ruinously expensive, but he had insisted on paying for it all himself—and the household expenses, too. He would not touch Grace's money.

Grace was in the sunken living room, sipping a cocktail and watching the crackling fire in the fireplace. She did not move when he entered, gave no sign that she knew he was there.

"I'm bushed," he said. He sank into a chair, stretched his legs out.

She didn't answer or look at him.

"What time are Mike and Doris coming?"

She said nothing.

"Grace!"

Finally she moved her head slightly, glancing at him out of the corner of her eye. There was the faint hint of a smile on her mouth. "Martini, darling?"

"A double," he answered. "A great big dry double."

"Yes, master."

She was gone for awhile; then he heard her moving around, fixing his martini. He felt dull and depressed.

"Here you are."

He opened his eyes, saw the martini in her hand, and reached for it. Then his hand stopped short. He stared at her noticing she had changed her clothes; now she was dressed in skin-tight black tights, sandals, and a sheer white nylon blouse. The blouse was almost transparent, and she was wearing nothing underneath it. She smiled down at him as she ran a hand across her nipples, hardening them.

"Like?" she asked.

"Not only do I like, I love."

"Here, drink your martini." She handed him the glass.

"I'd rather—".

"Oh, Dr. Regan!" She turned and walked away, deliberately swinging her hips. "You're so blunt, so basic."

"Grace, what in hell is going on?"

"Why, nothing, darling."

She had turned in front of the fireplace, facing him again. Her breasts were beautifully molded, the nipples erect, tantalizing. How many times and through how many nights had he. . . ?

"When are they coming?"

"Soon," she answered. "Too soon for what you have in mind."

"Then why this show?"

"What show?"

She was smiling at him, deliberately teasing him, something she had never done before. Sex had always been a magnificent thing with them. A mutual thing, coming from both of them. It was something that happened between them, made them contented and happy and tired, and now she was acting like some neurotic tramp, dressed the way she was, displaying herself and at the same time denying him.

"All right," he said, "you win, Grace. I don't understand what it is you're trying to do, but it'll keep."

"Of course it will, darling. It always keeps. We

don't have to worry about it spoiling, do we? You'd better hurry with your dinner."

"I guess so."

"You don't mind eating alone, do you? I want to stay out here by the fire."

He stood up, draining the last of his martini, and as he looked at her, a horrible idea came into his mind.

"You are going to change, aren't you? I mean, before Mike and Doris get here."

She smiled but did not answer.

"Grace, you can't dress that way in front of them."

"Why not? I'm sure they both know what I look like."

"Oh, for Christ's sake!"

"Don't be angry, darling."

He was angry, and he realized this was just what she wanted. What in the world had got into her? Why was she acting like this?

"I'm sure Mike will appreciate these," she said, still smiling. "Doris is so flat-chested. The poor man probably never gets to see what a real woman looks like any more. You know, before they were married, Mike was quite a gay dog around our fair city. He even propositioned me once. I was quite flattered."

"I refuse to let you do this, Grace."

"Why, Dr. Regan, that's not very progressive of you. We're living in an enlightened age."

"Damn you, Grace!"

He turned and strode out of the room. He went to their bedroom at the back of the house. He slammed the door behind him. He stood in the darkness, fighting himself, trying desperately to control his anger.

34

He was an intelligent man, a psychiatrist, a man who dealt in problems like these every day. So why could he not solve this one?

Regan only dimly remembered how he had got through the last few hours sitting at the card table, dealing, playing, listening to the polite conversation around him—steadily drinking one brandy after another.

By the time Mike and Doris had arrived, Grace had somehow transformed herself into a typical loving wife. She had also, at least, put on a brassiere under that flimsy blouse.

Mike Hartnell was small and stocky, heavily muscled, always neatly dressed. He was an insurance salesman—money and sports cars were his obsessions.

Doris Hartnell was taller than her husband, quiet and subdued, pleasant-looking only because of years of the best beauty care that money could buy. She was Grace's oldest and best friend. She was very thin, in spite of having given birth to four children, and her stylish clothes hung on her, as if no amount of money could make up for her scrawny frame.

The bridge night had become a regular, once-a-week ritual among the four of them. Mike was intense in bridge as in everything else, and he usually won. To Doris, bridge was only an excuse to see and talk to Grace; she was an automatic player with absolutely no variation in her game.

Regan was ordinarily a good player, but tonight he simply went through the motions.

Finally he heard someone say, "It's after midnight," and then someone else: "My God, I'm tired." Chairs scraped back. There was a little talk. Then silence.

Regan was finishing the brandy when Grace came into the room.

"They've gone," she said.

He rose, swaying slightly.

"You're drunk," she said. "I've never seen you drunk before."

"I'm going to get drunker," he told her.

"Why?"

He stared at her. "Why in hell not?"

"Paul, you were rude to Doris tonight."

"Hell with Doris!"

The look on her face was one of complete, incredulous shock.

He left her and went into the kitchen, hunting for something to eat. He found some cheese and crackers, and hooked up the coffee pot. He did not intend to get any drunker, despite what he had told her; he knew he was acting foolishly and he had to pull himself out of it, sober himself up.

An hour later, after the cheese and crackers and three cups of coffee, he went into the bedroom.

The bedside lamp was on. He could hear water running in the bathroom. He stripped off his coat, tie and shirt, sat down on the edge of the bed. God, he was tired. He would have to get away; before too much longer, he would have to take a trip somewhere, perhaps even go back to see Dr. Bemelman again.

There were so many places he wanted to go. Perhaps the happiest time of his life had been that year after the war—wandering through Europe, not caring about anything, just living from day to day, and yet being happy. It had been before the great influx of American tourists had spoiled things. He tried to remember the name of the small village in Belgium, near the Ardennes, the hunting lodge just outside the village. The name escaped him, but he could clearly remember the Belgian family that owned the lodge—the man and his wife, both short, fat and red-faced, and their brood of children, all fat and red-faced, too. Strange, he thought, that he and Grace had never discussed the possibility of having children.

Jesus, what is the matter with me?

He slowly removed his shoes. He was getting in too deep, far too deep—he was allowing himself too much self-pity. What if he was having trouble with Grace? Men had trouble with their wives; it was a normal, everyday occurrence, as normal as . . .

The water had stopped running. He heard the bathroom door opening, the soft, soothing sound of Grace's bare feet against the rich carpet. Then she came into view. She sat down in the bucket chair in front of her dresser. She had on a pink terry-cloth robe. She sat with her back to him, steadily brushing her hair. He could see her face in the mirror—her puzzled, worried expression. This was his wife, his woman, the woman for him—and whatever else happened or had happened, she would always be his woman.

She turned to look at him, still brushing that beautiful reddish-brown hair. "Are you feeling better now? Are you over your childish pout?"

"I'm feeling fine," he said. "How about you?"

Her stroking became angry. "Oh, hell," she snapped. "My hair is a mess."

37

"Your hair is never a mess."

She threw the brush at him, and he had to duck away to keep it from hitting him.

"Damn you," she said. "Damn you to hell, Paul Regan."

She rose, slowly, sensuously, letting the robe fall away from her, and he sat looking at the beauty of her body—knowing what he knew about it, everything there was to know about it. His eyes swept along the beautifully molded thighs, across the smoothness of her stomach, up to the thrusting cones of her breasts. She was biting her lip as she stood there slowly swaying her hips—teasing him, urging him. A sound came from deep in her throat—then he was leaping across to her, enfolding her, and they were together in their mutual hunger.

4

SOMETHING had wakened him. He lay in the dark, listening, eyes still closed. He could hear a gentle rain falling outside. He reached a hand across, slowly, feeling for Grace, wanting the touch of her. His hand came away empty, and he sat upright in bed. He switched on the bedside lamp, looked at the clock: it was twenty to five.

He shook his head and got up.

He walked barefooted down the hall into the living room. Grace was sitting naked in front of the fireplace. There was no fire in it now, and he thought she must be cold. He walked over and sat down beside her on the floor.

"Are you warm enough?" he asked.

She said, "Yes."

"It's raining outside," he reminded her.

"Yes." Her voice was subdued.

He tried again. "It's cold in here."

"I'm not cold," she said.

"All right. Do you want me to build a fire?"

She turned her head and looked at him, her eyes

shadowed in the semi-darkness. She put a hand out touching his shoulder briefly.

"That was the best," she said.

"Never better."

"Are you sure?"

"Grace, I'm positive."

She crossed her arms under her breasts, crouching, as if she were freezing.

"You are cold," he said.

"Not really."

"Thinking big thoughts?"

"Thinking no thoughts."

"Sometimes that's best."

"You are so intelligent, doctor."

"Not always."

"You are so right."

Regan wondered how long she had been there like this. There was a dry taste in his mouth, and he remembered the brandy he had drunk.

"Did you bring the painting home?"

For a moment, he wasn't sure he had heard correctly. He let it sink in, and alarm welled up inside him. He fought against it. She could not lapse back again—he would not let her.

"You're cold, darling," he said. "Let's go back to bed."

Without replying, she rose to her feet and left the room. He followed her into the bedroom. She was standing in the middle of the floor, waiting for him.

"Tell me about the new one," she said harshly.

"What new one?" He sat down on the edge of the bed, thinking dully, *Here it comes. Now it starts all over again.*

"The new one that was in the office tonight," said Grace.

"She's not a patient of mine," Paul said.

"What was she doing there, then?"

"She came to see me, at the request of someone else. She's having—troubles. She won't be back."

"Did she sit on that couch?"

He knew what couch she was talking about, and was sorry he knew.

"No. I don't think so. What difference does it make?" Perhaps this was the way—talking calmly like this, answering her questions. "She's a social worker, a very intelligent young woman."

Grace's hands were holding her breasts now, squeezing them, deliberately hurting herself, pointing the nipples at him, symbolically accusing him of something, he knew not what.

"Are hers bigger than mine?" she demanded.

"I don't know, Grace. It wouldn't make any difference."

"Are they as beautiful as mine? Do they taste—"

"Grace! How long is this going on?"

"Mine are beautiful, aren't they?"

"They're gorgeous. They're wonderful. I've told you that a thousand times."

"How many women have you had, Paul?"

"Oh, God!"

"That's no answer. That's no answer at all."

"What do you want me to say?"

"I want you to tell me the truth. Isn't that what you demand of your patients?"

"I'm not a patient of yours. I'm your husband. I wish you would remember that. I wish you would

41

get that stuck in that beautiful little head of yours, get it in there and leave it in there and never let it out. Grace, what I do with my patients, what I feel with my patients and what I say with my patients, has nothing whatever to do with you. You are you and I'm I, and the people who come to me are sick, actually sick, and I try to help them, the best way I know how. I am not involved with any of the women who come to me, no more so than any other psychiatrist would be; I do not want to make love to these women, sleep with them. I only want you, desire you. Can you understand that? Can you get that through your head?"

"Yes."

"Good. Then let's go to bed. It's almost time to get up and I've got a long day facing me tomorrow."

"All right, Paul."

Later, he had no idea how much time had passed— he was conscious of the rain still falling outside, of her breasts against him, of the feeling that there were only two people in the world. . . .

Her voice was a soft murmur in his ear. "Paul, darling, you didn't answer about the painting. Did you bring it home? You remember, darling. We were going to burn it and stick pins in it. You do remember, don't you, darling?"

He said, "Yes, I remember," and there was a bitter taste in his mouth.

"Did you bring it?"

"I forgot it. I'll bring it tonight."

"Promise me, darling."

"I promise you."

42

Why had he lied—what good would it do? Perhaps he had been hoping that if he put it off long enough, Grace would forget about the painting. But as he lay there, sleepless in the dark, he knew—grimly and bitterly—that she never would.

5

HE WAS LATE getting into the office. He had left Grace still asleep, had stopped on the way to have breakfast. He felt nervous and worn out. There was that thin wire stretching between him and Grace, stretching, stretching . . . How far could it go before it broke?

Sara, fresh and alive-looking, was sitting behind her typewriter. Her good-morning smile turned into a frown. She said, "You look tired, Dr. Regan."

"That a nice way to greet me? But I am tired. I'm bushed."

"Why don't you take the day off?" she suggested.

"Don't be ridiculous."

She looked hurt. "I'm sorry. I apologize for intruding into your thoughts. They're none of my concern."

"Oh, Sara," he said, sinking into a chair. He looked at her. She was wearing a tweed skirt, low-heeled shoes, and the usual tight-fitting sweater. Her sensitive brown eyes looked at him trustingly, and then she turned away again, poking at her neat brown hair.

"Sara," he went on, "you're the salt of the earth. I'm sorry I spoke so sharply to you, just now. I'm using you as a scapegoat for my own troubles."

"That's all right, Doctor," she said, appeased.

"It isn't all right. It isn't fair to you."

She smiled coquettishly. "I'll complain—at the proper time and in the proper place," she said. "Don't you worry about it."

Regan sighed. "I could use some coffee."

"It's perking."

Sara kept a coffee pot in the office, kept it going all the day.

She added, "Dr. Werner called. He would like to see you sometime this afternoon, if you're free."

"Am I?"

"After four, yes. Jeanne Higgins is due this morning at ten, and Mrs. Michaels this afternoon at two."

"Is that all?"

She smiled. "Yes, that's all. It should be enough."

"Good. It sounds almost like a vacation."

"You need one," she said.

Regan grinned. "Don't analyze the psychiatrist, please."

"My intentions are of the highest."

They laughed together, easily and naturally. He was grateful for Sara—she was a help to him in more ways than one. She reminded him a little of Pamela—he wasn't sure why. Lately, he had been depending upon her more and more. She seemed almost his only bridge to normalcy. Thinking back, he could trace the beginning of this feeling to the time Grace's jealousy had begun. More and more, he had been using his relationship with Sara as a buffer between himself and his patients . . . between himself and his wife. The insight worried him. He should not be doing such a thing to this girl—it was unfair.

"Sara," he said, "you should be married."

She got up and went to the coffee pot. "You seem to forget that I was married."

"We're all entitled to one mistake," he said lightly.

She shrugged. "A nice theory. If you look at it that way, I've made mine. I don't wish to make another."

"One man is not all men," said Regan.

"I don't wish to discuss it."

She crossed the room and handed him a steaming cup of coffee. Their fingers touched, momentarily and he felt her abrupt withdrawal at that moment. Could she be frightened of men?

"And so," he said, "you spend your lonely nights watching foolish movies."

"Dr. Regan, all movies are not foolish. I enjoy them. I know they are a form of escape for me, but each of us does need some kind of escape, regardless. Even you."

"I'm sorry, Sara," said Regan contritely. "I shouldn't interfere in your life."

"Besides, my nights are not lonely. How would you know about my nights?" He was acutely aware of the steadiness of her gaze. "I have many interests," she went on. "A great many interests. I am living a life of my own choosing, completely, and there aren't too many people in this crazy world who can say that."

Yes, she was right there. He nodded to her ruefully and took his coffee into the other room. In a way, he supposed he envied her. After all, how did he know how she spent her nights? For all he knew, she might have a dozen panting young men on the string.

He shrugged, and sat down behind his desk. He took a pipe from the rack, filled and lighted it. He certainly should not be thinking about Sara now; he had far too many other things on his mind, including his own problem, Grace.

Jeanne Higgins was due in at any moment, and he wanted to listen to the tape recording of yesterday's session. He switched on the recorder beside his desk, leaned back and listened, trying to blot out everything from his mind but the sound of her voice, the careful interruptions he had made. . . .

Jeanne was always exactly three minutes late—it never varied—and she always made exactly the same entrance, hasty and confused, as if she had just the briefest of times to spend with him between two important meetings.

Today, as she came hurrying into his office, almost flinging herself forward, she said in that quick-running voice of hers, "It rained last night and I love the rain. Did you see the rainbow this morning, when the sun finally came out? It was beautiful, absolutely gorgeous, stunning, breath-taking. I sat there and looked at it and wondered about it and wished I could make myself a rainbow, have one for my very own, just so no one else could see it. I wouldn't share it. It would be mine alone. Mine. Do you think that's

wrong, to want something like that for my very own?
I don't think it's wrong. I don't."

"I don't either," Regan said quietly.

She sat down in the chair opposite his desk. She
folded her hands primly in her lap, her knees close
together, like a child waiting in the principal's office.
She would sit that way for ten minutes, and then they
could officially begin the session.

Jeanne Higgins was twenty-six. Although Regan
would not have admitted it, she was his favorite
patient, because of the challenge she presented. She
had been referred to him by a psychiatrist in Los
Angeles, where she had lived before coming to Beach
City.

"I don't know," the psychiatrist had told him, "I
really don't. She consulted me for almost a year and
she is, without a doubt, the most complex human
being I've ever met. I haven't even been able to
diagnose her problems yet, though I know she has
a great many. Sometimes, sometimes I feel she's
laughing at me, at what I stand for."

Jeanne was of medium height, rather stocky, with
heavily muscled forearms, the result of a weight-lift-
ing fad she had gone through. Her hair had changed
from brown to brunette, to red, in the weeks she had
been consulting Regan—it was almost an orange-red
now, glaring bright. Seen in profile, her face was
strikingly beautiful, with its long, Grecian nose and
full, pouting lips. It was only when she turned full-
face that the beauty was lost—the slight puffiness in
the cheeks became more apparent, the full lips became childish, almost absurd. Her blue eyes were

48

big, rounded, childlike, fascinating in the way they changed with her mood.

She was the only daughter of Anne Higgins, a movie siren of the thirties, and Mark Harrison, a still-famous movie producer and director. She had refused to take Harrison's name; she wanted nothing to do with him, though it was his money that supported her in a lavish style. "I'm not even sure he is my father. He says he is. He's such a ghoul, really, tall and creepy, with that goddamned long nose and those funny little eyes and the way he never smiles, absolutely never smiles. I simply can't imagine Mama going to bed with him, doing that with him—I simply cannot get a clear picture of that. No! I don't think he is my father and I don't wish to even think about him." Her mother, now dead—killed in an airplane accident in Baja, California with a drunken football star—had married five times, had been famous for her wildness—Harrison had been her third husband. Jeanne's birth, if you could believe her, had been an accident; her mother, according to her, had had seven previous abortions. Jeanne had been unwanted, disliked, unloved by either parent —shifted from place to place, school to school.

She did nothing with her life, absolutely nothing. She was supposedly writing a book, but Regan could not find out what it was about. She had traveled all over the world. Eventually she had settled in Beach City and leased a house on the beach, a huge monstrosity that must have cost Harrison a fortune to maintain. ("I need the peace and the quiet. My God, I long for the peace and the quiet, the chance to be alone with myself and think about me all the time and look at the beauty of that goddamned Pacific Ocean.")

If he could believe her, she had had no fewer than fifty-eight affairs, ranging from a jockey ("He was the cutest little thing, really; you just can't imagine!") to a weight-lifter ("My God, you should've seen those muscles!"). She was trying to outdo her mother, who had told her that she had slept with two hundred and twenty-seven men and then lost count.

Her choice of clothes, or rather lack of choice, was fantastic. Nothing ever fit her; nothing ever matched. It was almost as if she had a mountain of clothing, piled somewhere in a corner, and, as she went by each morning, she took what was on top.

This morning she was wearing a man's coffee-colored trench coat, tightly buttoned, hanging almost to her ankles, and a pair of dark suede pumps with high heels.

She smiled a vacant smile at Regan, sighed deeply. "Well, I feel much better already."

"I'm glad."

She turned, looking around the room, while Regan switched on the tape recorder.

She shook her head. "Something is different in here. I can sense it. Have you changed the furniture around?"

He remembered about the painting, then. It had slipped his mind. He wished he had not given it to Jessica Hopkins the night before. It had been an impulsive, foolish thing to do, but it was done—he certainly could not ask for it back.

"The painting," he said, "that I had over the couch."

"Oh? It's gone. I am sorry. I was so fond of it. What happened to it?"

"I gave it away."

"You didn't!" She grinned, waving a forefinger at him. "You dog, you. I'll bet you gave it to some pretty girl. Now, don't deny it. I won't hold it against you. Really, I won't. That's your privilege, and you can do that if you want."

"I've done it."

"Of course." She shrugged in the huge raincoat, clutching her sides. "It's goddamned chilly in here. Can't we have any heat? I'm certainly paying you enough to get a little heat."

"Certainly." He got up and crossed to the thermostat. He touched the thermostat dial without moving it, then went back to his seat.

"There," she said, "that's much better, so much better. I don't know. I've been simply freezing all morning. That goddamned rain ruined everything, simply everything."

"I thought you enjoyed the rain."

"Did I say that?" she demanded.

"Yes, you did."

"Well, I didn't mean it. Not in that way. Actually, I abhor rain. It's so messy. It messes everything up. It makes mud, and I hate mud. Mud is so—so dirty, don't you think? So muddy. It ruins everything. The sand was all wet this morning and I wanted to take a stroll along the beach and look at the waves, and commune with nature, and then that goddamned rain rained all over hell and I couldn't take my stroll. My day is ruined."

"What about the rainbow?"

51

"What rainbow? What are you talking about?"

"Nothing. It doesn't matter."

"If it doesn't matter, why did you say it? Oh, I know all about you, Dr. Regan, all about you. You don't fool me a bit, not a bit. You think I'm some kind of a nymphomaniac, don't you? I'm not. I just like sex, that's all. There's nothing wrong with it; you ought to try it a few more times and find out a little. There's nothing bothering me, absolutely nothing. It's just that I have nothing better to do with my time, so I come in here and sit down with you. I like to talk to you, I really do. Have I ever told you that before? I must have. Incidentally, what do they call a man who can't get enough sex? What's the word?" She shook her head angrily. "It's getting goddamned hot in here all of a sudden. What's the matter, haven't you got any blood in you? It's the blood that makes you get up and go, isn't it? Let's cut out that heat or I'm going to go right up in heat."

He got up and went through the motions of adjusting the thermostat once more. This, too, was a never-varying pattern with her.

"I'm very tired this morning," she announced.

"Why don't you lie down on the couch?"

She thought about it. "Will you smoke your pipe for me?"

"Don't I always?" he asked.

"I guess so. I can't remember."

She rose and walked around the room while he filled and lighted his pipe—another little ritual of hers. She had to touch everything in the office, as if to verify that these things actually were there, that they actually existed. When she had finished with this, she turned and said, "This office has always reminded me of something. I can never remember what, though. Maybe one of these days."

She came toward his desk. "Will you help me with my coat?"

He got up to help her with the raincoat. He was unprepared for what he saw when he slipped it off her shoulders. Underneath she was wearing the bottom half of a bikini—and nothing else. She smiled at him coyly over her shoulder.

He returned her smile hesitantly and hung up the raincoat. When he came back and pulled up a chair beside the couch, she lay down, legs apart, hands cupped behind her head. Her big, childish eyes stared into his face, as if she were desperately trying to read his thoughts. Her breasts were small and round, the nipples disproportionately large, as if they did not belong to her, as if someone had merely loaned them to her for decoration.

"I'm so tired," she whispered, licking her lips.

"You probably aren't getting enough rest," Regan said.

"But I am. I'm sleeping ten hours a night."

"Then why are you tired?" he asked.

"I wish I knew." She put a thumb in her mouth, sucked on it for a moment, then pointed the wet thumb at him. "Why don't you like me?"

"I do like you."

"You never try anything. You never make an approach."

"That doesn't mean I don't like you."

"Mama always said it did. She always said that. She said that if a man wouldn't make a pass at you he was either queer or else he didn't like you. You're not queer, are you?"

"I hope not."

"I didn't think you were. You don't look it, though sometimes you can't tell. I got stuck that way once. You know something?"

"What?" asked Regan.

"I haven't been with a man in almost two months. That's something of a record for me. I can't remember when I've gone that long before. Mama never went that long—I know she didn't. She couldn't have gone that long."

"Then that makes you a little better than she was."

"Does it now? I don't think so. I need a man. I really do. Last night, I was home alone, reading this book, and I got all hot and bothered. You know how it is. I went out, intending to get a man. I met this Army captain. He was a nice enough guy, I suppose. He had this real cute little mustache, sort of painted on. We drank some and danced some and he tried to wiggle around on the dance floor with me and he was panting to beat all hell—but nothing. I didn't like the way he kissed me. It was like being kissed by a—I don't know, a seal, maybe. My God, he didn't even know how to kiss me." She blinked rapidly. "I bet you'd know how to kiss me. I bet you would."

"I probably would."

She opened her mouth wide, pointing the tip of her tongue at him, waving it back and forth like a flag. She paused to say, "Why don't you try?"

"I can't."

The tongue darted in and out. "Why not?"

"I've told you before. We don't need to go into it again."

"Hell, your wife wouldn't care." She shook her head, pouting. "All right. Your pipe's out."

"I know."

"You look so manly, smoking a pipe. He smoked a pipe."

"Who?" Regan asked.

She pouted.

"You know."

"But I don't."

"I told you about him before," she said sullenly.

"I guess you did. Tell me about him again."

"I can't even remember his name. I have a hard time with names. I used to write down their names in a little book and write a little bit about each one of them—you know, what they liked to do, and how, and all that."

The minutes ticked by slowly. He raised his head a moment and looked at the blank space on the wall where the painting had been.

Jeanne was talking again, her voice droning on and on, something about the man who had smoked the pipe, the nameless man.

". . . his clothes always had these little holes in them. I used to laugh at him, laugh at the way he would almost burn himself up. Mama thought it was rude of me to laugh at him. She scolded me, but he said it was all right, that I didn't mean anything by it. Where were we living then? Did I tell you? Oh, yes. We were up in that goddamned castle on the top of some lousy mountain, and there was a war of some kind going on. I remember that. There were all these soldiers and sailors and marines around, all the time. You couldn't go anywhere without seeing them, and Mama always said they were a stinking nuisance.

"Anyway, he was always burning holes in his clothes, all the goddamned time. One night, Mama left the house and I knew he was in there alone and so I went in there and he was lying on the bed with all his clothes on, just lying there, staring up at the ceiling, and I sat down on the edge of the bed, and he asked me what I wanted. I told him I just wanted to look at him, that was all, just look at him. He laughed at me. He lay there and laughed at me, and said I was certainly my Mama's child all right. I didn't like him laughing at me, but I sure liked looking at him. He had the softest hair, sort of fluffy, sort of sticking out all over his head and I had seen him one time brushing it, the way Mama always brushed her hair. That time, that time when he was on the bed, I put my hands in his hair and felt how soft it was and he told me I shouldn't do such things, that people wouldn't understand, that Mama wouldn't understand if she came in. I didn't care. Pretty soon, I was kissing his hair and he was laughing and giggling and rolling all over the bed and I was having a real good time. I was enjoying myself."

She blinked up at him. "Mama didn't like it, though, just like he said. I don't know how she found out about it, but she did. I guess he told her. He just sat there and smoked that pipe and looked like a wise old owl and all the time Mama was getting madder and madder. She said I didn't know what I was letting myself in for, and she'd show me. She

56

did—with his help. She thought it was the first time I'd ever seen anything like that, but it wasn't.

"I wish I could remember his name. I started writing the names down after that. I always wanted to remember his name. It was sort of like the first time for me, although he never did do anything to me, but I always felt like he did. I dreamed about him for years and years. But I could never remember his name or what he really looked like. I just remember that he was big and smoked that pipe all the time and had that fluffy hair. I asked Mama what his name was once, years after that, and she slapped me across the face and had her Japanese servant throw me out of the house.

"I wonder why she did that. Could you tell me?"

Regan cleared his throat.

"There could have been many reasons. Jealousy, perhaps. I didn't know your mother."

"But you must have seen her."

"Of course. Many times. She was—well, when I was growing up, she was a symbol."

"Did you think she was beautiful?"

"I suppose, yes."

"Sexy?"

"Very much so."

"Sexier than me? Prettier than me?"

Regan didn't answer.

"Why don't you like me?" she insisted.

"I do like you."

"Kiss me, then."

"I can't."

"I know. Maybe that's why I want you to." She

57

opened her mouth again, flicking her tongue in and out. "Just once. Could I kiss you?"

"The same thing."

"No." She grinned. "If I ever got my mouth on yours, got my tongue in you—" She laughed loudly.

"Let me think about it."

"I'd rather act than think. Thinking is for people who don't know any better."

"Why do you say that?"

"Hell, it's much more fun to do it than think about it." She swung her bare legs around, sat up on the edge of the couch. "I'm not getting very far with you. I usually do better than this."

"That's not your purpose in coming here," Regan said.

"To hell with my purpose in coming here!"

"Then perhaps we'd better cut out these sessions."

"No!" There was an anguished look on her face.

"If you need a man, if you need sex, there are plenty of men around to oblige you."

"But you're different."

"I said no."

"That's what the other head-doctor said. I had him before it was over. I'll have you, too."

He tried to smile. "Not now, at any rate."

"I do need a man. I'm almost sick for want of a man. I'll get one tonight."

"If that's what you want, it shouldn't be difficult for you."

She got up. "I'd better go."

"The same time Monday?" he asked.

"Is it Friday already?"

"I'm afraid it is."

58

"A whole weekend ahead of me." She laughed, hugging herself. "I have a new interest. I'm reading Roman history."

"An interesting subject," Regan said.

"Very. Especially the part I'm reading. They had the greatest love customs. Wow! I want to tell you all about them. Maybe we could—"

"Next week."

He got her raincoat and helped her on with it. She pushed herself deliberately against him, smiling that childish smile—whispering an obscenity, just loud enough for him to hear. He didn't react, merely led her to the door and watched her leave.

He went back and lay down on the couch.

Where was he going with her? Where could he go? Where could he lead her?

For the first time in many months, he was beginning to doubt himself, to wonder just why he had chosen the field of psychiatry. What was there in it for him? A selfish question; but he had a right to be selfish, a perfect right.

He was asleep within five minutes.

He slept peacefully, untormented by dreams—slept soundly, so that he could not see Sara come in, smile down at him, place a cool hand against his forehead. He stirred slightly when she did so, causing her quickly to withdraw the hand.

Then she was gone, and he slept on.

6

REGAN went home early that afternoon, without stopping to see Dr. Werner. He did not feel like seeing anyone, least of all a fellow psychiatrist. His afternoon session with Sheila Michaels had gone very smoothly, much better than the morning session with Jeanne. Sheila was progressing nicely; there was hope for her.

It was still daylight when he drove into the garage, the first time he had been home that early in weeks. He parked his car and sat for a moment, his hands still gripping the steering wheel, his thoughts idling. What would Grace be like this time? Would she bring up the painting again?

There had to be a point somewhere at which they could meet, could end this ridiculous battle. There was no sense in it. Grace was not even possessive toward him—she had never been that way. He remembered their first date, a week after that cocktail party. . . .

They were having a late dinner at Margo's, a

fashionable restaurant at the end of the pier, near the amusement park. Not many diners were there at that hour. Grace and Regan had a table by the window, where they could see the moon glinting palely on the water, hear the gentle lapping of the waves against the pilings below.

"I probably shouldn't tell you this," she said, smiling mischievously, "but I was waiting for your call. I wanted you to call me."

"You knew I would," said Regan.

"Yes, I guess I did."

Regan found out what schools she had gone to. He learned about her interest in golf and how she had won a trophy at the club when she was only sixteen, and then had never entered the tournament again. How she had been madly, desperately in love at fourteen with a friend of her brother; how her brother was adventurous, always going off to some distant corner of the globe to build a bridge or a road . . . so many things, big and little.

That first night, their first date: he realized he was day-dreaming like a lovesick adolescent. Well, why should he be ashamed of it? They had talked on and on, each finding in the other something he had been searching for. Later, in the darkness of the car, with the deep darkness of the night around them, with the trees and the gigantic shadow of a house looming outside their tiny world, he had kissed her for the first time, gently, lovingly.

There had been nothing more than that, then. . . .

Someone was shaking him by the shoulder. He came out of his stupor and saw Agnes standing out-

61

side the car, reaching in at him, shaking him. There was a deep concern in her dark face.

"You all right, Dr. Regan?"

"I'm all right, Agnes."

Agnes was the Regans' part-time housekeeper, a woman of uncertain age, round-featured and happy. She had a tendency to mother Grace and Regan.

"I seen you sitting out here, Dr. Regan, all alone."

"I was just thinking."

"You been sitting there a long time."

"Have I?"

He got out of the car. He was surprised to see that it was dark out. The house lights blinked invitingly across the expanse of lawn, welcoming him.

How long had he been sitting here?

"You sure you're all right?"

"Yes, Agnes. I'm positive."

"Mrs. Regan ain't home," said Agnes, following him out of the garage.

Regan stopped. "Where is she?"

"She went to play golf this morning. She ain't been home all day. I can stay and fix some supper for you."

"That's all right, Agnes. I'll manage."

She shook her head. "Dr. Regan, you don't look so good."

Regan turned to look into the garage. Why hadn't he noticed before that Grace's car was gone? Perhaps he was over-tired; perhaps he . . .

"I knowed a doctor like you one time, worked for him a couple months." Agnes' voice was coming to him as if from a great distance. "He was a nice gentleman and everybody liked him. But he worked and

62

he worked and he worked and he never took no time off and one day he just up and died, right on the spot."

"I'm not about to die, Agnes."

"You're a mighty tired man, Dr. Regan."

He walked away from her, only vaguely aware that she was still talking. He did not want to listen to her; he did not want to listen to anyone.

Inside, the house seemed too big and too empty. Grace had not wanted so large a house. He remembered, with an abruptness that almost shocked him, sitting in some gigantic railroad station when he was a child, just sitting there on the cold, wooden bench, waiting, waiting . . . what had he been waiting for? It was late at night and the station was nearly empty. An old man with a dirty beard was sitting across from him, chewing tobacco, occasionally spitting on the floor, and a baby crawled along the floor through the spittle, and some woman screamed words he couldn't understand at the dirty old man. . . .

And now he was alone in this big house, tired and alone, dejected, worn thin. Perhaps he needed a rest.

He walked from room to room, turning on the lights as he went, until he came to his den. There he did not turn on the lights, but sank down into a chair and closed his eyes.

He heard Grace moving around in another part of the house, calling him. He waited, not answering, and then she was framed in the doorway, the light behind her.

"Paul?"

"I'm here."

"Couldn't you hear me calling you?"

"I guess I was asleep," he said.

"Are you all right?"

"Of course."

"Agnes said you weren't feeling well."

"Agnes is a poor substitute for a doctor."

"May I come in?"

"A silly question."

She laughed uncertainly as she came into the room. She bent down to kiss him lightly on the forehead, then moved on and sat on the couch. She lighted the lamp beside her, and he saw the stack of unread books on the floor. Perhaps he could get back to his reading later tonight; he had nothing else planned.

Grace stretched and yawned. She was wearing a pale blue pullover, a plaid tweed skirt, brown-and-white golfing shoes.

"A good day?" he asked.

"A fair day."

"I haven't played golf with you in weeks."

"You don't have to tell me that."

"How about tomorrow? We could play together."

"Paul, I can't," she said.

"Why not?"

"I promised Doris I'd go shopping with her. She has to buy new outfits for the children and you know she simply has no taste at all."

The telephone was ringing. The insistent sound reached him from another part of the house. He stirred momentarily, but did not get up.

"Shall I answer it?" she asked.

"No."

"It could be important."

"To hell with it. Nothing is that important."

64

"One of your patients might—"

"And to hell with my patients. Tonight I am not in the mood for any of my patients."

"That's not a very professional attitude, doctor."

"And to hell with professional attitudes."

"My, my," she said, and laughed.

The phone had stopped ringing.

"They should invent a substitute for the telephone," he said. "Something that wouldn't remind you there's someone on the other end, sitting there, waiting for you to answer."

"Your conscience is bothering you now."

"I don't deny it."

"You can't do anything about it."

"Not now. It's too late."

She was looking intently into his face, her eyes serious, probing. "Paul, I love you. I love you so damned much. Sometimes . . . sometimes, it's almost more than I can stand. Today—" She shook her head, looking away from him. "Today, it was misting slightly when we were playing. The mist felt good. I sliced my drive on the eleventh hole, into those trees, and I was over there, looking for my ball and, suddenly—darling, you don't know how sudden it was—I was thinking about you and the time we got caught in the rain on the beach. I wanted you with me right then. I was being foolish, but I wanted you with me." She grinned. "It's silly, and I suppose a wife shouldn't say such things to her husband, but that's what I felt."

"It isn't silly, sweetheart. It never is."

"You haven't called me that in—ages."

65

"Sweetheart, sweetheart, sweetheart. There, that's enough to keep you happy for a while."

She came over and sat on the floor beside him, put her arms around his legs and rested her head against his thigh. He put a hand on her head, feeling the softness of her hair. For a while they were content to stay that way, without moving or speaking. Then Grace raised her head, "I have an idea."

"Will wonders never cease!"

"Don't be funny. You fix the martinis, and a fire in the living room, and I'll cook up some dinner and we'll have it in front of the fire."

"A wonderful idea."

"Kiss me."

He leaned down and kissed her, letting his mouth tell her of what he wanted. Desire welled up inside him, almost overwhelming him, and then she was pushing him away from her, laughing.

"Not now, darling. Later." Then she rose to her feet, almost dancing out of the room. "Dinner in forty-five minutes," she called back.

Regan's weariness had left him. He got up, went into the living room, and began to build a fire. Grace had always liked a fire, even when it was too warm for one—there seemed to be something about an open fire that made her feel relaxed and secure.

Dinner before the fire—could she be remembering that night so long ago? He hoped so. She was not sentimental as a rule—it was not like her to cling to a certain song or a certain place or a certain happening as a symbol of their lives together. But she had mentioned that rainy evening on the beach. And now, perhaps, she was recalling that night—the crackling fire, the dinner.

It had been three nights after their first date. He remembered the way she had looked, standing there outside his office building when he came out. It was a comfortable warm evening, with just a hint of a breeze coming in off the ocean, and people on the street were moving lazily—no one was in a hurry.

"I've been waiting for you," she said. "If you have any plans, you'll have to change them."

"Just like that?"

"I insist. You have no choice."

She stood there with her hand on his arm, her eyes looking into his, ignoring the people who were passing on either side. He sensed what she was offering him.

"I'm going to cook dinner for you. I'm an excellent cook. We're going to be alone, just the two of us, and you're going to tell me why you are what you are and I'm going to tell you the same. And then we're going to make love. I know that—I want that. And afterward, in the darkness, we'll be there together and we'll make our plans for the future."

She was that simple and direct, and Regan was stunned. He had never known such a woman before.

They drove to her cottage on the beach north of town. There was a curious silence between them. Regan half-resented her self-confidence, her taking him for granted. And yet he could not have said no.

The dinner was excellent. Everything was perfect— the table setting, the food, the wine, the soft music, the fire with its warmth and its pale glow. There was hesitant small-talk between them—and then he realized that she was really frightened of what she was doing—frightened but going through with it anyhow.

And then afterward—that first time, on the carpet in front of the fireplace, their lovemaking was shocking in its primal intensity. In all his life, he had never felt anything like that.

Later, as they sat on the floor with their backs against the couch, in the half-darkness, she asked if she had satisfied him.

"More than I could ever tell you," he said.

"You are probably thinking that I'm a very loose woman."

"I'm thinking nothing of the kind. What went on before me has nothing to do with us."

"Spoken like the intelligent, reasoning gentleman that you are. But I want you to know, Paul. This isn't the usual thing with me. I can imagine how many women must have told you that. But in my case, it's true, and it's very important for you to believe that. There have been only two men for me, and one of them actually was a boy, when I was sixteen. The other—well, the other was a man, pure, unadulterated man, and I took from him what he took from me and there was no love between us. Do you believe that?"

"Yes."

"Simple. Now, that's out of the way. You know me and I know you. We will never know each other more than we do at this very moment, Paul. There is nothing left for us to do but share our lives. . . ."

"Are the martinis ready?"

68

He looked up to see Grace standing there. "I've been daydreaming about the past," he said.

"Nonsense. Blonde or brunette? No—" she waved a hand at him— "Don't answer that. This is no time for daydreaming."

"I'll fix the drinks," he said.

He was mixing the martinis when the phone began ringing again. They glanced at each other—then Grace answered the phone. She smiled ruefully as she handed the receiver to Regan.

"Yes?" he said into the phone.

"Dr. Regan, this is Charlotte Hendersen."

"What is it, Charlotte?"

At the sound of the name, Grace turned quickly, staring at him. She was holding an unlighted cigarette.

"I can't seem to get in touch with Dr. Werner," the voice said. "He prescribed a tranquilizer for me and the stupid druggist will not refill the prescription for me without an okay from the doctor. I'm in a bitchy state, Paul. I need that prescription. Could you—would you call the druggist?"

"Charlotte, I have no idea whether or not Dr. Werner would want you to have a refill on it. If he had, he probably would have marked the prescription that way."

"Damn! You won't help me?"

"I really can't, Charlotte."

"Was that Grace who answered the phone?"

"Who else would it be?"

There was a strange sound, as if she were scratching her fingernail across the mouthpiece. The voice said, "She's a jealous wife, Paul."

"Is that all, Charlotte?"

Grace was staring at him. He could see the tiny muscles moving in her face. She was getting angrier by the moment.

"I miss you," Charlotte said plaintively. "Dr. Werner isn't—"

He put down the receiver.

"Damn that woman!" Grace said.

"She's sick, really sick. We have no right—"

"She has no right calling here." Grace looked at the cigarette in her hand, then tapped it angrily on the table.

"She needed help," Regan said.

"She could have called Dr. Werner."

"She couldn't get in touch with him."

"So she said. You hung up on her, didn't you?"

"Yes."

"Why, Paul? What did she say that made you do that?"

"Let's not discuss it."

"She must have said something to make you hang up on her."

"Please, Grace. I don't feel like discussing it."

"But I do."

"Is this going to spoil our evening?"

She hesitated, and he noticed that she was shredding the cigarette in her fingers. She looked down at it, as if she had just realized what she had done.

"Damn her," she whispered.

"It isn't her fault, Grace. You must realize that."

"Why isn't it? You're my husband. You don't belong to her. She can't call you any time she feels like it and discuss me."

"What?"

"Don't play innocent! I know her. She's a bitch and a whore, and she had no right calling you with her problems. She can't keep her pants on, that's all."

He sighed. The tiredness was returning. Slowly, surely, it was creeping back into him.

"All right, Grace," he said. "You win. Charlotte Hendersen was a patient of mine before I even knew you. I can't help that. She is mentally disturbed and I was trying to help her. I think I did help her—at least, I identified her problem. As often happens in a situation like this, she identified herself with me too strongly. That's why I recommended her to Dr. Werner for therapy. I felt he could do a better job with her than I could, under the circumstances. You've known this all along."

Grace did not seem to be listening to him. There was a blankness in her face, as if she were mentally somewhere else, in some place of torment. It was a look he had seen many times in the faces of his patients, a look that frightened him now.

"Grace!" he said sharply.

Her eyes flickered. "What?"

"Charlotte means nothing to me. You've got to realize that. I know it's hard for you. I suppose you see a lot of Charlotte at the Club, and I know how malicious she can be. But your love for me has to—"

"That's enough!" Grace stamped her foot angrily. "You don't have to tell me about my love for you."

"I hope not," said Regan.

She threw the torn cigarette into the fireplace, turned her back to him. "Are the drinks ready?" Her tone was different, more composed.

71

They drank the martinis, and tried to forget the phone call, but it was no use—the mood was gone. The evening was spoiled and they both knew it.

Their emotions were stretched so taut. He wondered how long their marriage could stand the strain.

7

THUNDER rumbled in the distance. A dog's lonely barking answered the sound, and Paul could hear the insistent patter of rain against the roof. He was wondering what it would be like if he and Grace were the last two people on earth. A stupid, sophomoric kind of thought, the kind of thing he had discussed so often in his undergraduate days. Just him and Grace. There would be no jealousies then.

Or would there? . . .

He was on the couch, his feet propped up, shoes off. Grace was sitting cross-legged on the floor, in a relaxed posture. They had talked little at dinner—both afraid of saying the wrong thing, of beginning their destructive quarreling all over again.

Grace raised her head. "Why don't you smoke cigars?"

He laughed, a little puzzled. "I don't like cigars."

"Why not?"

He laughed again. "I've never analyzed it. I just don't like them."

"You're the kind of a man who would look good smoking a cigar."

"That's a nonsensical statement if I ever heard one."

Dimly, somewhere in the back of his mind, a warning blinked on. There was something familiar about this conversation. Somewhere, at some time, another person had spoken to him about cigars in much the same way. Was it possible that he was mistaken? He lay there, searching his memory. The connection was teasing him, just beyond his reach.

"Really, Paul." She turned slightly, gazing at him. "I think you would look very distinguished smoking a cigar."

"Well, I don't like them, and that's that. My smoking habits are my own affair."

She ran a hand through her soft hair, loosening it. "When were you in Paris, Paul?"

"At various times, during the war and after—the last part of nineteen-forty-six and the first part of nineteen-forty-seven."

"Did you like it?"

"I loved it."

"I loved it, too."

He sat up. The rain was coming down in earnest now, drumming hard on the roof.

"I never knew you'd been to Paris," he said.

"Haven't I ever mentioned it?"

"Not that I recall."

"I was there. It's a fascinating city—evil, sensuous, like a woman made for the one obvious thing."

Again, the words she used struck some chord of memory inside him.

74

"I was alone," she went on, in a curious, unnatural voice. "And I was searching. You know how young people search. My life here had been regulated, forced into a boring pattern—I wanted something different. There was a tourist guide at the hotel where I stayed. He was young and very dark, and because he was so young he smoked cigars, and they made him look foolish.

"There was another American girl staying at the same hotel, a college student on tour. This guide, his name was Louis, he took this other girl and myself on a drive in the country one sunny afternoon. We drove and drove through the quiet afternoon, and we talked. Louis wanted to be a writer—he wanted to come to the United States. Most of all, he wanted to see Hollywood, see the movie stars. That was his whole life.

"Anyway, we were miles from Paris and the sun suddenly disappeared, and it started to cloud up and then to rain. Louis' car was a convertible, but he had no top for it. We stopped in this little village and went to the hotel there, The man who owned the hotel knew Louis, and we had a great feast in a little room on the second floor. There was a fire in the fireplace and we could see the street down below, the water running in the gutters. I remember seeing a little boy and his dog, walking along in the rain, loving it. It was all very romantic, this other girl and myself and Louis.

"Paul, something happened then that I'll never be able to explain, not to you or to anyone else. It was sex and passion and everything basic, everything animal, within us human beings. The three of us—" and

75

she was looking directly into his face then, staring into his eyes—"we stayed in that hotel room for four nights and three days. We had no idea of the time— we had no idea of anything but each other, what each of us wanted. I sampled everything there was to sample, Paul . . ."

He was listening to her, frozen, and yet not believing her—he could not believe her.

As she talked on and on, he could not believe that this was his wife, that this woman staring up at him, talking so vehemently, so filthily, miring herself deeper and deeper in the sordidness of perversion, was actually Grace. It was as if someone else had pushed her aside—as if some foul trick were being played on him—as if he were being punished for some crime.

And at the same time it was all familiar, so naggingly familiar, as if he had heard it all before—

As if someone else had told him the same story . . .

Of course! He slapped his hands together suddenly. "Grace!"

She stopped. She ran her tongue around her lips.

"Grace, what in hell is this? What kind of—"

"It's awfully hot in here, Paul," she said.

She pulled her sweater over her head, tossed it on the floor, then unsnapped her brassiere. Her breasts burst loose, tantalizing. She cupped them in her hands. "Two at a time," she murmured, smiling. "The greatest thing in the world. Two at a time kissing them."

He shook his head.

"Do you mind if I lie on the couch?" she asked.

"Where did you hear this horrible story?"

76

"It's my story, baby," she said. She had never called him that before. She laughed. "Please, Paul, I would like to lie down. The confession has tired me. I need to lie down."

"It's not your story, Grace. It can't be."

"And why not?" She was fondling her breasts.

"It's impossible. You couldn't have done such a thing. Besides, I've heard it before."

"From whom?"

He hesitated. He was not sure; he could not be sure. So many stories from so many patients . . .

"Are you going to let me lie down or not?" She demanded.

He got to his feet. The fire was low, and he put another log on it, watching the sparks fly upward. Damn, was he going out of his mind? This evening simply did not make any sense.

"Louis looked so foolish with that cigar. But he was so adept in so many other ways. I think you would look wonderful with a cigar, baby."

It was like a record going through his mind, over and over and over again. So many patients, so many years. Which one?

"That was the most exhilarating experience of my life, baby. We could—" she giggled—"We could—"

"Damn it! Stop it, Grace. Stop it this moment."

"You remind me of Louis, in a way. You're much older, of course, and you're so much more handsome. But there's a likeness between the two of you. Perhaps we could get someone else, maybe Charlotte, and—"

But he was through listening. He walked out of the room, out of the house, ignoring the rain that beat

77

down on him, knowing only that he had to get away from her, from those eyes, that droning voice.

He got his car out of the garage and drove aimlessly down the wet streets. There was little traffic. The things Grace had said kept going through his mind, over and over.

Where? Where had he heard them before?

And then, suddenly: *Charlotte* . . .

She had mentioned Charlotte.

Of course.

It all came back now. Charlotte Hendersen had told him the very same story. He should have remembered it before. Anger welled up in him, making him twist the wheel suddenly. The car skidded sideways on the slick paving. He felt the front wheel hit the curb and swung the steering wheel back. Something scraped solidly against the side of the car, and then he was all right again, driving slowly.

He remembered Charlotte telling the story now—he even remembered the circumstances. She had stripped to the waist, just as Grace had done, and she had asked about lying on the couch. She had talked about cigars and had suggested that perhaps they could do what she had done before, get someone else. . . .

It was hard to believe. Charlotte had come back a long way. She was bi-sexual, torn between the two sexes—unsure of herself, unable to cope with her desires. He remembered, now, Sara's mention of Dr. Werner—that Werner had wanted to see him this afternoon. Perhaps it had something to do with Charlotte. She had called tonight, obviously on a pretext—wanting to talk to him.

He looked around to see where he was. He was only a few blocks from home—he had probably been driving in circles. There was a lighted gas station on the corner. He saw the phone booth at the side of the station and pulled in.

A man came out of the station office, waved to him. "Hi, Doc. Wet night."

He waved back and entered the booth, searching his pockets for change. He dialed Dr. Werner's home phone. There was no answer. Then he dialed the answering service.

"I'm sorry, Dr. Regan," the woman's impersonal voice said, "but Dr. Werner flew to San Francisco this evening. He won't be back until Tuesday."

Regan hung up and slumped against the side of the booth. He should have dropped by at Werner's this afternoon. But he had been tired and discouraged.

Excuses meant nothing. The fact was, he had made a mistake.

He looked through the book for Charlotte Hendersen's number. She was divorced. When he knew her, she had been living alone in an apartment near the University. He found her listing, dialed the number. She answered almost immediately.

"Charlotte," said Regan grimly, "what have you been telling Grace?"

"I don't know what you mean, Paul."

"Damn you, Charlotte," he said, "don't play games with me."

"You sound angry," said her distant voice.

79

"I am angry."

"I'm being honest, Paul. Believe me, I have no idea what you're talking about."

Regan paused a moment to control himself. "You said something before, when you called, about Grace's jealousy. Now, what have you been telling her? What have you been doing to her?"

He heard her laughter. "Grace has been making a perfect fool of herself at the Club. Don't go by what I say. Ask the others. She's done everything but physically attack me, and I'm not so positive she won't try that one of these days. And she's been lamming into Margaret Simms as well."

Regan saw that his hands were shaking. He would have to take hold of himself—he could not afford to go around primed for trouble this way. He had no proof, really, that Charlotte had told Grace the story. It seemed to him it was the only thing that could have happened—but accusing Charlotte like this, without any conclusive evidence, would get him nowhere.

"All right, Charlotte. I'm sorry I disturbed you. Accept that for now, please."

"Baby, you didn't disturb me. I'm all alone."

"Good night, Charlotte." He started to hang up.

"Paul?"

"What?"

"You're not home, are you?"

"What difference does that make?"

"Why don't you come over here and tell Mama Charlotte all about it? You've listened to my troubles for so long. You've helped me. Now maybe I could help you."

"I appreciate the offer," Regan said. "But no."

"Any time, baby. The door's always open."

He hung up. There was a continual whirring sound in his head—it would not go away. He remembered being a child, going to the county fair. There had been a ride, something on swings that went 'round and 'round, swinging him high above and beyond the world, propelling him into space. He felt the same way now, as if he were swinging high up somewhere and there were no way down.

The station attendant was standing beside his car, running his hand along the side. "You sure as hell ran into something, Doc."

"I know."

The man was looking at him curiously. The water was streaming down the attendant's thick-lensed glasses. He removed them to peer near-sightedly at Paul's feet. "You feeling okay, Doc?"

"Of course."

"You ain't got no shoes on."

Regan looked down at his feet. The man was right —he was standing in a pool of water in his stocking feet. He had left the house in such a hurry, he had forgotten his shoes.

"You been drinking, Doc? Want I should drive you home?"

"I'm okay, thanks. I—it was an emergency. I had to leave the house quickly."

"No phone there, huh?" the man said.

Regan got into the car, conscious of the man still peering at him. He knew this would be a topic of conversation for a long time. Dr. Paul Regan, the

81

head-shrinker, going out in the rain without his shoes. A lot of people would laugh. Yes, they would.

The house was dark when he got back. He found Grace in bed, asleep. She was on her back, arms outstretched in supplication. He wanted so much to help her, to help himself. The hole they were in was getting deeper and deeper and soon they would not be able to climb out of it.

He went to the guest bathroom, stripped down. He soaked in a hot tub for almost an hour, just lying there, letting his mind go numb. Everything was such a jumble, so mixed up. Nevertheless, he did not feel helpless, though it occurred to him that he might be. He had always been able to face whatever life offered, face it squarely and accept it. Dr. Bemelman had told him he was so normal that he was almost a freak. "You should share some of that normalcy with others, Paul," Bemelman had said. "It seems such a crime for you to have so much of it."

But was he really normal now? A senseless, useless term—meaningless. What was the norm? And what did Regan want? He wanted happiness for himself and Grace and he wanted to do what he had set out to do, and—so many things.

How could Grace have heard that conversation between himself and Charlotte? Of course, he recorded all his interviews on tape. But the tapes were locked in his office, tucked away in a filing cabinet that doubled as a safe. Grace could not have access to them.

Yet there could be only two possibilities: Grace had heard the story either directly from Charlotte or from the tape—or was there a third possibility? Could he have, somehow, repeated the conversation himself? He could have talked in his sleep; he could have, unknowingly, supplied her with the conversation. The possibility was there, however remote.

But his mind kept coming back to Charlotte Hendersen. Something in him kept insisting that it was she who was guilty. She had said hysterically that her love for him was the only thing that kept her going—she had wanted to possess him, his body as well as his mind, and he had refused her. It was not the first or last time that a patient had fallen in love with him. There was usually an identification of some kind; there had to be. But Charlotte's had been abnormally intense. That was why, for her own good, he had had to sever the relationship. Could she still feel vindictive enough toward him to be capable of a thing like this?

8

SATURDAY morning was sunny and warm, delightful after the night's heavy rain, with the sun streaming in the bedroom window. Bits of fog still clung to the ocean below, like white puffs of cotton along the shimmering blue-green.

Regan had awakened in an angry mood, determined that Grace would have to accept him as he was—that he would accept no more excuses for her.

Once, after breakfast, as he was reading the morning paper, smoking his first pipe of the day, he felt her hovering near him.

He looked up. She asked, "Where were you last night?"

"I went out," he replied curtly. "That's all you need to know."

She turned and left the room without a word.

Regan worked a couple of hours in the backyard, trimming hedges, adding to a brick fireplace he was making—losing himself in the immediate physical labor of what he was doing. Once he saw Grace standing at a window, looking out at him. He deliberately ignored her. He was being childish, he realized, and yet he could not help it.

When he came in from the yard, she was waiting in the living room, dressed to go out. Even then, feeling as he did, he was struck all over again by her beauty. Whatever happened, Regan knew that she would go on being for him the most beautiful and desirable woman in the world.

"I'm going shopping with Doris," she told him. "Will you be here when I get back?"

He slumped into a chair. "Where else would I be?" He looked away from her. He did not want to remember the way their life together had been. It would never be that way again, and he might as well accept the fact.

"Paul?"

"What?"

"For what it's worth, I'm sorry."

"You've said that before."

"Paul?"

"I can hear you."

"Help me. Please."

He hesitated. She was pleading so sweetly and sincerely with grief in her voice. But how long would her mood last this time? How long would it be before she reverted to what she had been last night.

"I don't think I can," he said heavily.

"All right."

The sound was so pitiful, so heart-wrenching, that he almost leaped out of the chair. He wanted to go to her, hold her, tell her that everything would work out—that all this was nothing but a horrible nightmare. But some force held him motionless in the chair—and then he heard her leaving and knew that it was too late.

The afternoon dragged by. He moved from room to room, almost like a sleepwalker, unsure of himself, not really caring what he did. He settled in front of the television set for an hour or so, watched a college football game.

Regan had been a good football player in his youth. He had followed his grandmother's advice. In high school, his name and fame had spread throughout the state. He could even remember the scrapbook his grandmother had kept of his exploits.

Damn! He was getting to be a middle-aged fool, sitting around in a lonely house, reminiscing about the past, about his glory days as an athlete. Yesterday was gone. He had to live for the present, for today.

For the first time, he began thinking of what would happen if he and Grace split up. The idea came as a shock. But it happened to others. It could happen to him. People would be surprised to hear that this perfect marriage, this ideal match, the one they had thought could never go wrong, had hit a snag, had turned sour.

What would life be like without Grace? Adjustment to marriage had not been difficult for him in spite of his long years of bachelorhood, and yet there had been definite changes. His life had grown to be regulated with hers. There was, of course, the physical presence of her as a woman, the fact that she was there when he wanted her. That in itself was terribly important to a man with his sexual needs. There had not been another woman for him since he had met Grace. Occasionally, he had seen someone—at a party, at the club or just walking along the street—who had made him pause and wonder what she would be like. But there had been no real desire on his part for another woman—Grace had been woman enough.

He had been in Beach City for a little over three years. Before Grace, there had been two or three women for him, the minimum necessity of relieving his tensions. Would he be forced to go back to that again? Knowing himself, he knew that he would, and he also knew that after Grace, no woman would be enough for him.

He also wondered, selfishly, what effect a separation or divorce would have on his standing in the community. He liked Beach City. And Grace was a Winston, with everything that the name meant in Beach City.

Somehow the hours slipped by, the afternoon waned, the sun disappeared and with it the warmth of the day.

Grace came home a little before six, still looking as fresh as the minute he had last seen her. She had that knack.

He had been reading a new biography of Mussolini, written by an obscure Italian journalist who had known him in his young days. It was mostly sordid stuff, the popular variety, dealing with Mussolini's relationships with women.

Grace came into the den, her face serious.

"Have you been working?" she asked.

"Reading," he said. And then: "Did you have a good day?"

"I suppose you could call it that."

He sat, thinking how banal their conversation was; they might have been two bored acquaintances meeting on the street. Before, there had been no need for this kind of talk. Now it seemed to be a bridge between them, their only link.

"Doris—wondered if we were still going to pick them up on the way to the Club."

He had almost forgotten about tonight, the dance at the Club.

"Are we going?" he asked.

"That's up to you."

He turned a page. "Why should it be?"

"Oh, Paul!"

He closed the book with a bang. "I suppose it would embarrass you not to be there."

"Since when have you—" She didn't finish whatever she had meant to say. Her eyes were angry now.

"Go ahead, say it."

"I don't want to say it."

"You're not being very consistent, Grace. Last night you said a lot of things."

"Last night was—different."

"What made it different?"

She turned away. "Don't cross-examine me!"

"Who told you that fantastic story? Where did you hear it?"

"What difference does it make?"

"We'll have to talk about it sooner or later."

"Not now. I've been—sick all day."

"Why?"

"Anxiety." She shrugged helplessly. "Who knows? I do know we're—we're doing horrible things to each other, saying horrible things to each other. I'm not sure how much more I can take."

"There are only two solutions."

"I know."

"We either try to go back to what we were, or—"

"Don't say it! I don't want it said!" She leaned against the door jamb and for a second he thought she was going to faint. The color left her face and her eyes rolled upwards. Then she slowly straightened. "Even if it happens, eventually, I don't want it spoken between us yet. Let's keep it unsaid."

"That's avoiding the issue. We won't solve it that way."

"Is there a solution?" She gestured wearily. "No! No, don't answer me."

"Maybe that's where most of your trouble is, Grace. You talk a lot, but you don't listen to me. When I talk, you close your ears, block me out."

"I suppose you're right. You're usually so right, Paul."

"Not always. But we've got to do something. This is ruining us. This is—"

"I don't want to talk about it!"

Grace almost screamed the words at him. She turned and he could hear her running down the hallway, then the sound of a door slamming.

He waited a moment before following her. She was in their bedroom, standing at the window, staring out at the darkness. She did not turn when he

89

entered, but he saw her shoulders stiffen, as if she were expecting a blow. What must she think of him?

"All right, Grace," he said.

"All right what?"

"There's little point in our getting angry at each other. We have enough problems without that."

"You're so right, Doctor."

He let her sarcasm pass.

"I'll go tonight," he said, "if you still want me to."

"Thank you for that. I've—" she turned slowly, her hands folded together— "I've worked hard on the committee. It's important to me."

Both the hard work and its importance to her were true, and he silently acknowledged it. Every year at this time, the Club gave a benefit dinner-dance at exorbitant prices. The profits went to needy families for Thanksgiving and Christmas. The cause was worthy, he admitted, and yet he had himself wondering whether or not the people involved were doing more good for themselves than for the needy.

But Grace had worked very hard on the organizing committee, spending long hours in the planning. For her not to be there, regardless of the reason, would make many tongues wag.

"I could make excuses for you," she said, "if you prefer not to go."

"I said I would go."

"I'm glad."

"Grace, we'll have to face it."

"I know." She smiled, hesitantly, a little of her old self showing through briefly. "Just give me some time. That's all I'm asking—for now."

"All right."

"Is this—some kind of truce between us?"

"Call it what you want."

She took a step toward him, hesitated, and then turned and left the room.

9

THE CLUB, a Georgian monstrosity on a hill overlooking the city, was surrounded by an eighteen-hole
golf course of luxurious greenness, two swimming
pools, a dozen tennis courts. Past the seventh hole
of the golf course, in the foothills of the mountains
that insulated Beach City from the hot desert to the
east, were the stables and the bridle paths that led
through the mountains. It was rough country up
there, uninhabitable, undeveloped. He and Grace
had ridden over many of those trails, camped out—
it was the kind of thing he had once liked to do, to
get away from the daily life he led.

The Club had been formed shortly after World
War II by a group of the younger members of old,
established families in Beach City. They were people
who had enough money to indulge themselves in an
establishment more select than the public parks and
beaches and golf courses. No formal name had been
given to it—it was simply called The Club.

Grace had become a member when she was old
enough. Paul had joined of course at the time of

their marriage. Their social life was almost monopolized by club functions and club people. To Regan, the Club was a fact of life. The majority of the members were not what he would call needed additions to his circle of friends; on the other hand, there were some members whom he both admired and liked.

They picked up Mike and Doris and drove to the Club in an atmosphere of strained silence. Mike commented on the damaged condition of the car, but Regan did not explain. Doris was obviously aware of their difficulties—just as obviously, she considered Grace to be completely in the right. Mike tried to make small talk about the possibility of their all going up to San Francisco for Thanksgiving, but no one responded.

They arrived late. It was a thing Paul had come to accept whenever they went anywhere with Doris —she was habitually and chronically late.

The ballroom had been over-decorated, as always. Gigantic balloons hung from the ceiling, pivoting slowly on long strings; a mural depicting a slum section of Beach City had been painted on one wall; tables with white linen cloths formed a circle around the dance floor, and an orchestra was playing.

Paul thought that a lot of money that had been wasted on trimmings would have been better spent directly in the slums, but he kept the thought to himself, knowing how hard Grace had worked on this project.

It was a night of dancing, eating and drinking . . . of pushing your way across the crowded dance floor . . . of seeing Mark Grayson, president of the Chamber of Commerce, get falling-down drunk . . . of hearing Shep Sanders, superintendent of schools, talk about the many more Mexicans and Negroes coming into Beach City and flooding the city schools, lowering the standards . . . of watching Bob Sinclair and Harry Wright, two scions of Beach City's oldest and wealthiest families, brawling in the middle of the dance floor . . . of watching a banker copping a feel . . . a night of confusion and noise, a night that would be looked back upon by many as a night of happiness, a night in which they had given of themselves to those less fortunate—a night of anger, hostility and frustration.

Paul was disgusted by the whole thing. He wished he had not come with Grace, wished he were not a member of the Club. His work dealt with unfortunate people, yet had nothing to do with charity. As for Grace, he was thankful to see that she, too, was disgusted; she had never been a woman who liked these affairs for themselves. She had been caught in a certain situation of birth and wealth and had made the best of it: that was all.

Around midnight Paul saw a familiar face beyond the crowd, near the French windows. It was Jessica Hopkins, looking alone and lost in that crowd—a child in an adult's world. Paul was alone at that moment, too. Grace and Doris had gone to the powder room and Mike was off somewhere trying to make a sale, so Paul moved through the crowd, elbowing his way a little roughly, until he reached her.

Jessica was dressed attractively, not quite in such high fashion as most of the other women. But she had better natural equipment than most of them—long, trim legs, sensuous mouth, full breasts. . . .

94

"Miss Hopkins, this is the last place I ever expected to find you."

She smiled in welcome and gratitude. "Don't you think I belong with the rest of—" she grinned, looking around her— "of the human species, Dr. Regan?"

"Of course, I do. But I didn't think you were a member here. I don't remember seeing you here before."

"I'm not a member. I came with Harold Stern. Our office is handling the distribution of the proceeds. These fine people—" and again she grinned— "are giving of themselves tonight, so here I am. The other half."

"It's not too disgusting, is it?"

"Not as bad as I expected."

"How do you mean?"

"The stories one hears about this place. You have no idea, doctor. The orgies, the depravities that go on up here on the hill. We mortals down below have come to look up to this place as Beach City's number one sin palace."

"Is it that bad?"

"Worse, believe me."

"Where's Harold?"

"Off counting the money somewhere, I suppose."

"How about a drink with me?"

"Am I safe?"

"The question hardly deserves an answer."

"Just one little one, then," she said. "My limit is three, and I've already had the first two."

"I wish more people here would keep to their limits."

"Dr. Regan," she said, so quietly that he had to

strain to hear her voice, "if you don't like it here, why come?"

The question surprised him. He turned, looking around him at the sea of faces, listening to the voices, some high and shrill, some demanding, some monotonous. What was he doing here? He saw Mike at a table nearby, waving to him, raising his eyebrows suggestively at Jessica. Regan waved back, thinking how crude most of the social amenities were. Someone spoke his name, a vaguely familiar face hove into view; his hand was grasped, pumped roughly, and a voice said something obscene. There was a great deal of laughter and then, above all the noise, he heard Jessica Hopkins say, "Let's get that drink," and her hand was on his arm, leading him away from the pack.

There was a short, carpeted hallway leading from the ballroom into another room which had been set up as a bar. Curiously, this hallway was empty as he and Jessica entered it. He stopped, making her stop beside him.

He shook his head. "Of all the goddamned idiots!"

"I repeat my previous question," she murmured.

"I don't know why I came. Who knows anything, now, at this time of night and amid these horrible surroundings?"

"Dr. Regan, you're tired. Why don't you sit down somewhere? Rest awhile."

How many people had told him he was tired in the last week? Looking into her face, he knew she meant well. They all meant well, he supposed. But they could not know the hell he was going through, the despair, the loneliness.

"I am tired," he said. "Sick and tired of the filth, the mire. They think because I'm a psychiatrist that I'm—I don't know, perhaps the great symbol of sex or something. I'm only a human being. I have the same wants and the same desires as everyone else. I'm not above anyone else."

"You don't have to defend yourself." Her voice was strangely soothing.

"Don't I?"

"You are what you are and that's that."

"A breath of common sense," he said, waving his hand. The hand struck something or someone, and he turned to see a man and a woman standing there, both half drunk.

The man said, "Who the hell you hitting?"

"I'm sorry. I didn't mean—"

"You lousy goddamned head-shrinkers are all alike. Think you can push other people around."

The man was short and pudgy, with heavy eyebrows and a florid face. He said something to the woman with him and she laughed. Her shrill voice was ear-piercing in the confined hallway.

"I oughta slug you one," the man snarled. "Show you what in hell a real man's like."

All the anger, all the frustration suddenly came to a head in Regan and, before he knew what he was going to do, his fist drove into the man's thick middle. The man's eyes bulged; he doubled over and sank to the floor.

The woman screamed.

Faces appeared at both ends of the hallway. Someone yelled. The man Regan had hit was sitting on the floor, holding his stomach with both hands and fighting for breath.

The woman yelled, "He attacked him! He attacked him!" She swung a heavy purse at Regan's head. He ducked, too late. The purse caught him on the temple, knocking his head against the wall. He was momentarily blinded—and then the purse was swinging again and he got under it just in time. Someone grabbed the woman, lifting her off her feet. She kicked out, skirts high.

Jessica said, "My God! Let's get out of here."

He followed her down the hallway, past the staring, accusing faces, and suddenly there was cool, fresh air, and nothing else. He slumped down on a cold cement step and put his face in his hands.

When he finally lifted his head, Jessica was still standing there, calmly smoking a cigarette. She leaned down to put the cigarette between his lips. He inhaled deeply, coughing.

"You're too intelligent to get involved in things like that," she said severely.

"Don't lecture me."

"Dr. Regan, don't think me presumptuous. I came to you for help, but—"

"But you think I'm the one who needs help?"

"That's for you to decide."

He rose to stand beside her.

He had no idea why, but he felt better. He had enjoyed hitting that man. Perhaps it was the basic combativeness that is latent in everyone—he didn't try to analyze it. He knew only that he had enjoyed it, and that out there in the cool freshness of the night air and with Jessica standing beside him, he felt much better.

He touched her arm. In the half-darkness she seemed unreal, more like a dream than flesh and blood. He felt the need to touch her, to reassure himself that she was really there.

"Thank you," he said.

"For what?"

"For being you."

She laughed. She had a distinctive laugh. He remembered that she had cried in his office and that the sound of her crying had been so different from Grace's. She was completely herself—a strong, beautiful woman. For the first time, he wondered what it would be like to take her in his arms, smother her mouth with his own, make love to her.

"I guess we all have our problems," she said.

"You said something like that before, didn't you? When you were in my office?"

"I might have. I can't remember. I'd rather pretend that I had never been to your office."

"Then we wouldn't have met."

"Perhaps we would have managed."

She put a hand against his face, soothingly, her fingers trailing along his cheek, then down to brush against his lips. The touch was exciting.

He reached for her and felt her body pliant under his hands and knew, at that moment, that she could be his, right there on those cold cement steps.

Then he heard a door closing behind him and the sound of someone moving down the steps.

"Paul?"

It was Grace. For the first time, her voice was not welcome. It was an intrusion.

"I'm down here," he said, finally.

He saw the two of them, Grace and Jessica, looking at each other with the automatic hostility of two beautiful and desirable women.

Grace broke the silence. "Is he all right?"

"Yes," Jessica answered.

"Are you going to stay out here, hiding?"

He realized that Grace was talking to him. "I'm not hiding," he answered.

"What else would you call it?"

"It was an accident, Mrs. Regan," Jessica said. "I saw the whole thing. It was stupid and senseless."

"I'm sure you did." There was an iciness in Grace's tone.

"Mrs. Regan, I don't think I like you."

"I don't know your name, but I don't think I like you either. You seem to forget that he's my husband. If you're in heat, I'm sure there are many other men around to oblige you."

"Her name," Regan said, "is Jessica Hopkins. And, for the love of God, she was only being helpful. Don't make anything more of it than that."

"I suppose it's Miss Hopkins," Grace said.

"You suppose correctly," Jessica said.

"I feel sorry for you, I really do. I know how it must be, having to search around for a man to supply your needs. But the next time you want a man, please choose someone else's husband. Mine is—"

"Cut it out, Grace!"

"Of course, darling. Anything you say."

Jessica turned to him. Her smile was dim and wan.

100

"I'm sorry about all this, Dr. Regan, truly sorry. Some people blow the simplest things up all out of proportion. Evidently your wife is one of those people. I feel sorry for you if this is her usual approach and I find it easier to understand your previous attitude. Good night, doctor. Pleasant dreams."

He stood silently, watching Jessica disappear up the steps. The night suddenly seemed cold and damp. He shuddered. What would he have done if Grace had not come out?

"Well," Grace said finally, "you've succeeded in making a complete ass of yourself."

"What do you mean?"

"The story of your standing in your bare feet in the rain last night is going all over the club. And now this. Kenneth Gross is a very important man."

"Who in hell is Kenneth Gross?"

"The man you attacked, beat up."

"I didn't beat him up. I only hit him once."

"Good for you. What are you trying to prove, Paul? He's a harmless, middle-aged man with a roll of fat around his middle. It certainly doesn't add to your stature here for you to attack him, or whatever you did."

"I don't give a damn."

"Maybe that's your whole trouble. You don't seem to give a damn about much of anything lately, me least of all."

"What a stupid thing to say!"

"What were you doing with her?"

"Nothing."

"You're lying."

"Okay, so I'm lying," said Regan with sudden

101

fury. "Okay. Okay. I wanted her. I wanted her very much." And as he spoke the words, he knew they were true. "Is that what you want to hear? She's more attractive than you, much more. I wanted to strip her down, kiss her, make love to her."

For a moment he thought she was going to hit him. She looked on the verge of it, and then she turned away, hunching her shoulders, and he thought he heard the sound of a sob.

"Go ahead and cry, damn you," he said. "Go ahead."

She didn't answer or look at him.

"You're the one who's making an ass of yourself," he said. "Damn you, Grace, you're driving me out of my mind with your jealousy. I don't know whether I'm coming or going with you. Go ahead, cry, cry a lot, and then come up with some more of that neurotic nonsense."

He realized that his hands were clenched tightly into fists, that the anger was overcoming him. He closed his eyes. He had brawled with a fat little man; he had been caught by his wife with another woman; he was yelling at his wife.

Where would it all end?

"Let's go," he said quietly.

She didn't answer him. But with child-like submission, she followed him.

10

IT WAS like a nightmare, like those dreams he had had during the war when he had been forced to kill. He had killed the two Germans easily. It had been a simple matter of survival—their lives or his. He had been dropped behind the lines to make contact with an underground group. The two Germans had spotted him, tried to take him. He had killed them so easily, automatically—he had done what he had been trained to do. And then, months later, he had awakened every night for a week, seeing the way one's face had been half-blown away by the bullet fired at close range; the way the other one had looked at him, dumbly, as if he could not believe what was happening to him. . . . He had killed before that, during the war, and afterward, and yet it was that one time that had bothered him the most.

Now this too was like a nightmare, like something from which there was no escape or concealment.

Grace was sitting at the foot of the bed, staring at him, her eyes empty, and when he awakened and sat up, she started talking. Again it had to do with Char-

lotte Hendersen. Again she mouthed all the obscenities. It was strange; she sat there, completely nude,
her hands folded calmly, and without any evident
emotion she went through another session Regan had
had with Charlotte. It was frightening, uncanny. He
sat stiff, made no sound, while she went on talking.

This time it was Charlotte and the time when she
was seventeen—the three football players from the
University. He remembered it well. She was remembering all the sordid little details. She had taken on
Charlotte's identity, and she was living through it
again, moment by moment.

It went on. He tried not to listen; he tried to block
the whole thing out of his mind, but he didn't suc-
ceed.

There was no escape for him, no place to hide. He
was forced to sit there and listen, and acknowledge
the fear that was in him.

When she finished there was silence, for only a
few minutes. Then, without warning, she was on him,
fighting him, trying to subdue him. She was like a
wild animal, beyond reasoning—he was being raped,
purely and simply. He tried to fight back and then,
strangely, found himself falling into the same pattern. Like her, he was all animal. They rolled over,
their bodies locked in a wild, breathless struggle of
passion.

He came out of the bathroom, running a hand
through his tousled hair, feeling the weariness deep
within him. Every muscle in his body ached.

"What are you doing in here?" her voice said.

He wasn't sure he had understood her. "What?"

She was lying under the blankets, her hair spread

104

out on a pillow. Her eyes were accusing. She had turned on the bedside lamp and now as she looked around the room, a confused expression came over her face.

"I told you, Paul," she said, "that I won't share the same bed with you as long as you chase around after other women."

That was true. She had told him that when they came home—and she had gone into the spare bedroom.

"You came to me," he said.

She laughed. "Don't be absurd. I'm not that hard up."

She had no idea of what had happened, of that he was positive. He was not at all sure that he knew what had happened. It had not been Grace who had come to him just an hour or so ago; that had not been Grace at all.

"I told you to sleep in the other room," she said. "I know," he lied. There was no use in arguing with her—he knew she would not believe him.

"Then what are you doing here?" she demanded.

"I'm not sure. I was restless, I guess."

"You can get your satisfaction with other women from now on. I don't want you touching me. God knows you've been having other women long enough. You can just go on having them, enjoying them."

"If that's the way you want it."

As he started for the door, she said, "You forgot your promise."

"What promise?"

As he turned to look at her, she rolled her eyes,

chuckling. "The painting, you silly, you. You promised me."

"I know I did."

"A man should never break his promise to a lady. We'll build the biggest fire ever."

"All right."

"And I'll stick pins in it. I hate that painting."

"Will you do me one favor, Grace?"

"Ask it."

"Will you go and talk to Dr. Werner?"

She sat up in bed, and the blankets fell away, exposing her breasts. She bit her lip and shook her head, then slammed the flat of her hand down on the bed. But she did not answer.

"Grace, I'm not sure whether you can understand what I'm saying or not. But you need psychiatric help. It's for your own good, for our own good."

"You want me," she said in a curiously stilted voice, "to go to another man and tell him all the things that those women tell you. Is that it? Is that what you want?"

"Yes. He could help you."

"And do the things with him that they do with you?"

Angrily, he started to speak, then held the words back.

"The way you help those women," she went on.

"Each of us is different, Grace. Everybody has different problems and they have to be worked out in different ways."

"You think I'm—sick—mentally sick."

"I think you could use some help."

For a moment, as he looked into her eyes, he saw

106

the woman she had been, the Grace he had married.

"All right, Paul," she said at last, shrinking back under the blankets.

"I'll arrange it for you."

"Whatever you say."

He watched her turn her head away. He stood there a few moments and then went to her. She had fallen asleep almost immediately. As always, he was struck by the beauty of her, the almost terrifying beauty.

11

SUNDAY was a quiet day. Grace, complaining of a headache, stayed in the bedroom. Regan puttered around the house, doing nothing in particular. Doris called, and he told her Grace was not feeling well.

He spent the evening reading, preparing his lecture for the following Tuesday at the University. He buried himself in his work, putting aside his own problems. He had convinced himself that it would all work out, that Grace would see Dr. Werner and that, eventually, their lives would return to what they had once been.

At eight that night, Grace came out of the bedroom and said she would like to go to a movie, just to get out of the house. He decided to go with her; they went to the neighborhood theater. The movie was a western with a lot of violence, a lot of poor psychology.

They sat through about half of it and then she said, "This is horrible. Even television is better than this. Let's get out of here."

In the lobby, as he paused to help her on with her coat, she said, "If I see many more of those, I really will be sick." And her laughter was hesitant at first, then more natural as he laughed with her.

"Well, obviously two very happy people," someone said at his back.

He turned—it was Sara. "Good evening, Dr. Regan, Mrs. Regan."

"Is this where you spend your Sunday nights, Sara?" he asked.

Smilingly, she said, "Some of them."

"Did you enjoy it?"

"Do you want my honest opinion?"

Grace, still laughing slightly, put her hand on Sara's arm. "Never that, please. No one could possibly have an honest opinion about that."

Regan noticed the way Sara's brown eyes quickly clouded over. Probably she had actually liked the movie—her feelings were hurt. Regan felt sorry for her. Standing there beside Grace, she seemed so small, almost shrunken, buried in the folds of a heavy raincoat. Her darkish hair was mussed, as if she had been running her fingers through it, while Grace was as perfectly groomed as always.

"Can we drop you somewhere, Sara?" he asked.

"The bus will be along shortly."

"Nonsense," Grace put in. "Let us drive you home."

"Oh, no! Please don't bother."

Sara seemed confused, even annoyed, at the offer, and Regan found himself wondering why.

He glanced at his watch. "It's only about nine-thirty," he said. "I hate to ask you, Sara, but if you feel up to it, I'd like to work on the book for an hour or so. That is," and he looked carefully at Grace, "if it's all right with you."

"Of course it is," Grace replied.

"I haven't anything else to do," Sara said, giving Grace an odd look.

They drove home, Sara sitting in the middle. Regan couldn't help noticing the way she kept moving nervously on the seat. As their thighs or shoulders accidentally touched, he could feel her withdrawing instantly, like a hermit crab retreating into its shell. What could her marriage have been like if she were so frightened of touching a man?

At home, shortly after he and Sara went into the den, Grace came in carrying a tray of coffee and sweet rolls.

"Now you two just take your time in here," Grace said, "and work as long as you want. Just remember that you both have to be at the office in the morning. I'm going to bed and read, and I won't disturb you any more."

Regan followed her into the hall, took her by the arm. "You can be damned nice when you want to be," he murmured.

"Darling, I'm—I'm all confused. My head is spinning. I can't explain the way I've been acting. I've been thinking all day. I think—seeing Dr. Werner would be for the best."

"I'm sure it will be," he said.

She kissed him lightly on the cheek, and he watched her walk away. With renewed hope, he went back into the den.

He lost track of the time as he dictated. Sara sat quietly and primly on the edge of the couch, as if she

110

were afraid of relaxing in these surroundings. It felt good to work, to sink himself into the book. How long was it since he had been able to lose himself in his work?

Later, he looked at his watch and saw that it was after midnight. He turned to Sara, still perched precariously on the couch. She looked tired, older than her years, sad and helpless. He saw the way she was looking at him and smiled.

"I'm awfully sorry, Sara," he said. "I had no idea of the time."

"You don't need to apologize. I'm so wrapped up in it that I don't pay any attention to the time. It's—it's wonderfully done, doctor. Magnificent. You explain everything so clearly that even I can understand it."

"It's only a theory, Sara."

"I know, but it's still—I can't think of an adequate word."

"I hope some publisher feels as you do."

He got her raincoat and helped her on with it. She turned to him, and he could see the sheen of tears in her eyes, the way her lower lip was quivering, and he wondered that she could be so frightened of him, so frightened of any man. Or was it fright? He wanted to hold her close, the way he would a frightened, lonely child, but she moved away from him.

"I won't bite you," he said gently.

She shook her head. "You don't understand," she whispered.

"Understand what?"

"Nothing. It's nothing."

He drove her home in silence. She lived in an old apartment building near the university, not far from

111

Charlotte Hendersen's apartment. The words *University Arms* were printed on the front door in tiny bronze letters. There were mailboxes on either side of the small, arched-in lobby. It was a place like so many others, the kind of place he had lived in himself when he was in medical school.

"Thank you," she said.

"I should thank you, for taking your night."

"I liked it. I like—" She didn't finish.

"You take tomorrow off. Tuesday too, if you feel like it. Relax, enjoy yourself. Do something for fun."

"I enjoy myself most when I'm working."

He shook his head. "Good night, Sara." He got back into the car.

She was still standing in that little lobby when he drove away.

There was a strong wind blowing and he could make out the shape of some high tree being bent by the strength of the wind. A car passed. Somewhere someone was listening to music, the sound of it floated through the night.

Grace turned over when he got into bed, pressing her body against him. He lay still, not wanting to disturb her, but feeling desire mount inside him—the old desire that only she could quench.

"They're yours, darling," she whispered in his ear. "Take them. Kiss them. Love them."

And her hands were forcing his head down, down, down. . . .

It was not like before, not like the last time. This time, she was Grace, his wife, and she knew what she was doing. She laughed once, high and piercingly. . . .

12

His Monday morning was entirely taken up by Jeanne. She made her usual entrance, her usual complaints about the head and the cold, about his smoking a pipe for her. But there was something different about her this morning, a subtle difference that he almost failed to notice.

She lay on the couch, smoking a cigarette. For once, she was fully clothed, in a sleeveless orange sweater that bared her muscular arms, and black capri pants, much too tight. One hand held a heavy handbag slightly off the floor, as if she were afraid to let go. She said, "I lived this weekend. Really lived."

"You've been alive for some time."

"You know what I mean, damn you. I told you I was going to get me a man and I got me one." She turned her eyes on him, searching. "He was a man. In a way, he was like you, big like you, dark hair like you, luscious-looking like you—made me want to gobble him right up." She laughed. "You look good enough to gobble, Mister Doctor-man.

"His name was Jack," she went on, "and he had a

113

tattoo in the goddamndest place. It said just one thing and I had to laugh when I saw it, but by God I did it, and it was really living, believe me. Oh, he was a man, a real man. He gave me a bath in champagne. You ever do that? I suppose not. You'd be too much of a prude. He drank the champagne too, like they do in Paris. He told me about it. This club, the waitresses are bare to the waist and you buy a bottle and they pour it over their shoulders and you drink it as it runs down. Good?

"You know something? You bore me. You really do. You sit there like some goddamn god or something and look at me and I get all queasy inside, wondering what it would be like with you. I never had to wonder before. No, sir. Not me. But you bore me; you never do anything. I hope to hell you treat your wife better than you treat me. You just sit there, like you're not even a man. Maybe Mama was right."

She pulled her sweater up suddenly, exposing her breasts, letting them bounce free. The nipples were swollen. He could see a fresh bruise mark on the left breast.

"How many men could sit there and look and not do anything? What's the matter with you, anyway? You should want them. You should get down here and take them, taste them."

"Cover yourself," he said, trying to ignore what he felt.

"Why? Do they bother you?"

"Miss Higgins, I'm a doctor, a psychiatrist—"

"You're afraid," she said.

"Don't be stupid."

"Just once. Just once, try. That's all."

114

She was holding her breasts in both hands now, pointing them at him and, try as he might, he could not take his eyes off those nipples. What harm would it do?

"Bite them, Mister Doctor-man. Go ahead."

He felt the sudden tautness in his loins, the sudden desire, almost overwhelming in its intensity, and he knew that she was winning.

He rose and walked away to the window, closing his eyes and his mind. What was happening to him? He was a psychiatrist; there had to be a clinical detachment between him and his patients. If he ever lost that, he was finished. But how much could a man take? Where was the limit?

He heard Jeanne coming up stealthily behind him. Her arms went around him, pulling him tight against her. He did not resist. Her breasts bored into his back—he could feel the hardness of her nipples even through his clothing. Her mouth came up along his neck, her teeth nibbling at the lobe of his ear, gently at first, then harder, hurting him.

He whirled, knocking her against the desk. She had removed all her clothing. Her thighs were long, strong-looking, desirable. She stood facing him with her mouth open, her tongue darting in and out, her hips grinding in a slow, sensuous rhythm.

"Don't be afraid," she whispered, "just take me. Grab me. Hold me, love me, bite me, hurt me. God-damn you!"

He felt the tumult of desire within him—fought against it. But he had let himself take Grace when she had been in a disturbed mental state. Why not now?—why not this one? He took a step towards her

115

—and she fell into his arms, her mouth searching his face, finding his mouth, the tongue probing deeper and deeper, her hips grinding against him, her breasts exciting him. And suddenly he saw what he was doing, almost as if he were standing outside himself. He pushed her away, roughly.

Her body thudded against the edge of the desk. She shrieked, and he saw there was blood on her lips.

"Hit me!" She screamed at him. "Go ahead. Hit me, you son-of-a-bitch! You're like all of them. Hit me!"

He was silent, trying to control himself. His desire was fading now, and he was bitterly ashamed of what he had almost done.

There was hate in Jeanne's eyes as she looked at him, deep and vengeful hate. She was balling her hands into fists, breathing hard, her breasts rising and falling, her nostrils dilated, and her voice was harsh and strident: "I'll kill you! I'll kill all of you!"

He was in control of himself now, and for the first time, he had an inkling of what was troubling her. He said quietly, "That would do no good, Jeanne."

"Wouldn't it?" Hate was still in her eyes. "Why not? Explain it to me."

"There are so many of us. You couldn't destroy all of us."

"I could try."

"You have been trying to destroy us, haven't you?"

"I will. You wait."

"But you can't, Jeanne."

Now he felt the satisfaction of knowing what he was doing—he could cope with this, he knew it.

He saw tears welling up in her eyes. They spilled

116

over, and then she was sobbing like a little girl, hands coming up to hide her face.

"Don't look at me," she groaned.

He held her close, letting her cry it out. "Mama," she was saying, over and over again.

He led her to the couch. She lay down with her hands still over her face. He put her sweater and skirt over her, covering her as well as he could. "It's all right, Jeanne. It's all right now."

"It was never her fault," she said, taking her hands away from her face. She stared up at him with tear-blurred eyes. "She couldn't help being what she was. She was born that way, just as I was. She was so beautiful—they wouldn't leave her alone—they all wanted her. She told me that. I can remember it. She told me that was all any man wanted, her body. And she told me that no man had ever really possessed her. She gave them her body, but nothing else. She said, 'I give them my body and I lie there and laugh at them,' and that was true."

She shuddered all over, then grew rigid. "I'll kill them all! God damn them! I'll kill every mother's son of them, every goddamned one!"

"Easy, Jeanne," he said, putting a soothing hand on her forehead.

"Don't tell me that. I know you."

"Who am I?"

"You're one of them."

"But I want to help you."

"And I want to kill you!" she screamed. Sitting up suddenly, she grabbed his hand, tried to bite it. He pulled his hand away barely in time.

117

She twisted around, slapping and clawing at him with both hands, screaming obscenities. One of her wild swings connected, numbing his face, before he could grab her wrists and hold her. Slowly he forced her to lie down again.

He felt her relax in his grip—then she closed her eyes and was breathing deeply, steadily. He knew she was faking sleep, but he was glad enough to let her do it.

"Will you smoke your pipe for me?" she murmured, opening her eyes.

"I will, if you'll do me a favor in return."

"What?"

"Lie here quietly, don't move."

She nodded.

He knew he was taking a chance in leaving her alone, but he wanted to get her a sedative. He got up slowly, watching her. She lay still, eyes closed, the faint hint of a smile on her mouth.

"Remember," he said, "you promised."

"I won't move. Scout's honor."

He went quickly into the smaller office. He was surprised to find Sara there behind her desk.

He said, "Get me a glass of water, quickly."

He found the sedatives, took the glass of water from Sara. She said, "I could hear her screaming in there. Can I do anything to help?"

"Nothing." He went back into the other room, closing the door behind him.

Jeanne was sitting up on the couch. He noticed that she had picked up her handbag and put it beside her.

"You promised me you wouldn't move," he said as he went toward her.

"Promises are for fools." She grinned and licked her lips. "I have a surprise for you," she said.

He stopped, holding the glass of water foolishly in one hand, staring at the revolver she brought up from behind her handbag. The round, black muzzle was aimed straight at him.

"I told you," she said.

Regan was frozen. He saw the way her finger was curled around the trigger, and knew with cold certainty that he was facing death.

"I'm going to kill you," she said. "I'm going to pull this trigger and the gun's going to go bang-bang and you'll be dead. I'm going to watch you die. I'm going to watch your blood run out of you and I'm going to laugh."

Regan's muscles tensed. He measured the distance with his eye—about ten feet. Could he get to her before she could kill him?

"Boom-boom," she said, and laughed.

"Jeanne, this isn't the answer." His voice sounded strange.

"Boom-boom," she said again, still laughing.

He took a step. He saw the gun come up, the finger move slightly on the trigger.

"Mister Doctor-man, why didn't you like me? Most men do."

He didn't answer.

"I know," she said, rocking back with laughter. "Oh, I know, I know, I know."

"You know what?"

"I'll get you, Mister Doctor-man. After you're dead,

119

I'll have you. I always get what I want. My Mama told me everything. It was you that killed her and you don't fool me a bit. You killed her, damn you. You!"

Regan threw the water glass, and leaped forward at the same time. He heard the glass break against the wall behind her. He landed off balance, tripped and fell to his knees. One hand just missed Jeanne's ankle as she scrambled out of the way. She was off the couch, out of his reach, the revolver still pointing at him.

She screamed piercingly, and then Regan heard someone else gasping behind him. He turned and saw Sara standing in the doorway, a fist shoved into her mouth, her eyes wide with fright.

Jeanne squalled, "Get over there, you! With him!"

Regan said, "Do as she says, Sara. Quickly."

Sara obeyed. Regan got up beside her, gripped her arm so tightly that she gave a little yelp of pain.

"This is better, much better," Jeanne said. "The two of you. Your name is Sara, isn't it?"

Sara was too frightened to speak. She nodded dumbly.

"Don't worry, Sara," said Regan. "She's not going to do anything with that gun—are you, Jeanne?"

"You'll see. Goddamn you, you'll see." She waved the revolver menacingly. "Kiss her."

"What?"

"You heard me. Kiss her."

He looked at Sara's face, saw the way her chin was quivering, saw the fear and horror in her eyes. He bent down, kissed her lightly on the cheek. Even then, terrified as she was of the gun, she instinctively pulled away from him.

"You call that a kiss? I want to see you kiss her. She looks like she could stand a good kiss. Put your arms around her, hold her."

He whispered, "I'm sorry about this, Sara," and put his arms around her, pulling her close. He bent his head, touched his lips to hers. It was a very sedate, prim kiss, the kind a man gives to his sister or maiden aunt. Sara's lips were two hard lines, unresponding.

Jeanne laughed hysterically. "Kiss her, you son-of-a-bitch! I want those mouths open, those tongues working!"

He tried, but Sara would give nothing in return. There was no time for niceties. He forced her mouth open and, so suddenly that it caught him completely unprepared, her mouth was working against his, her tongue seeking, probing.

He could hear Jeanne's mad laughter even as he felt the passion that was in Sara. Then she was biting him, clawing at him; he tasted blood. He wrenched himself away with an effort, turning his head, forcing himself not to look at Sara.

"Good. Pretty good," Jeanne said. "Did you like it?"

Neither of them answered.

"That's good, for a beginning. Now, strip down."

"Jeanne, you must see how foolish this is." But he knew it was like talking to a wall. He could not get through to her.

"You might as well die in the saddle," Jeanne said. "That's the way my Mama died. Did you know that? She was having at it in that airplane. Strip! Right now!"

Sara was already pulling off her sweater. He looked at her and saw a glint in her eyes, a curious expression he had never seen there before. Was it possible that she was enjoying this?

Sara unhooked her brassiere, dropped it to the floor beside her sweater. She was blushing, furiously biting hard on her lower lip, but staring directly into his face.

"Take me," she whispered, "take me and love me. Please, please, please. I want you. I want it. Please."

Her breasts were incredibly big. He had never seen any that big, and they had huge, swollen nipples. He looked at them, half fascinated, listening to Jeanne's raw voice. She was telling them what to do. She was not leaving anything to their imagination.

And he knew that he could not go on existing as a man if he let this thing happen.

"That's enough, Jeanne," he said. "There won't be any more." He took a step toward her. "You'll have to pull the trigger, Jeanne." He took a second step.

Jeanne stood pointing the revolver at him, holding it with both hands now. He could not tell whether she was laughing or crying—maybe both. She pulled the trigger.

It took Regan a moment to realize that there had been no explosion, that he was not hit.

Jeanne threw back her head and laughed. She was pulling the trigger over and over. Regan realized that there were no cartridges, that the firing pin was striking against empty chambers—that she was laughing at him—that the whole thing had been some perverted joke.

Relief flooded through him. He was suddenly aware that he was soaked through with perspiration.

Regan had given Jeanne a sedative, and now she was asleep on the couch. He picked up the phone, called her father, Mark Harrison.

Quickly, but as gently as possible, he explained what had happened. "I think she is beyond my help for the present, Mr. Harrison," he finished. "I would recommend a private institution, where she could receive much more individual help."

"You must be nuts," Harrison said angrily. "There's nothing wrong with her. She's like her mother was. She just likes sex a little too much—" And he went on, villifying Jeanne's dead mother.

It sounded to Paul as if Mark Harrison could use a little psychiatric counseling too, but he kept that thought to himself.

Grudgingly, at last, Harrison agreed to have someone at the office within the hour to take Jeanne home.

Regan took another look at her now, lying peacefully on the couch, curled up in a fetal position. She had been unwanted, unloved. Who was he to blame her? But he knew that next time, the gun might not be unloaded.

He shuddered at the remembrance of the fear that had been in him when she had pointed the revolver at him. Death had been that close.

He thought of Grace—he should call her. If he had died an hour ago, if he had never been able to see her again—how would she remember him?

He went into the other office. Sara was standing

rigidly with her back to him. He saw her flinch as he walked into the room.

"Go home, Sara," he said. "Take some time off. Rest for a few days."

"I guess—I will," she said, without turning.

"I'm sorry you had to see that, be a part of it."

"It was my own fault, butting in the way I did."

When she turned, he saw that there was a redness around her eyes, as if she had been crying.

He hesitated, not knowing exactly how to put what he wanted to say. "You know that I was—forced to kiss you like that?"

"You don't need to explain it to me. Let's just leave the whole thing right there, please. I'll chalk it up to experience, and forget it. There was nothing either of us could do. I—the reason I took my clothes off—" She shook her head, looking at the floor.

"We don't have to talk about it, Sara. You go on home now, rest, forget about the whole thing."

She left without another word.

And Regan kept remembering how she had looked at him. She had wanted him. She would have gone through with the love-making, whether or not Jeanne had been there with the gun.

It was a curiously disgusting thought.

13

GRACE went back on her promise to see Dr. Werner. "I don't see the point in it," she told him. "There's nothing wrong with me that you couldn't cure, Paul. We both know that. It's you and those women. When you decide that I'm woman enough for you, things will get better for us—and not until then."

Regan came to dread going home at night. His nightly arguments with Grace were draining him. He could never be sure how she would greet him. The occasions when she was herself were growing rarer and rarer.

He drank too much. He was losing weight—his clothes were too big for him. Sara had returned, more subdued now, more aloof, and yet she could not always keep her thoughts to herself. "You've got to do something, doctor," she said. "You can't go on like this."

His thoughts kept returning to Jessica Hopkins—he wasn't sure why. There had been something defiant about her, something that had struck a spark of sympathy in him. He remembered that night at the Club—her calmness, the way she had kept herself apart from the others. He lay awake at night, thinking about her, wondering what she was doing.

But he knew he could not make the first move in her direction.

They met, finally, by chance. It was almost a month after the crisis with Jeanne Higgins. Regan was tired from his long day, and he didn't want to go home.

He stopped at a bar near his office and ordered a drink. Sitting on the bar stool, staring at his reflection in the mirror, he hardly recognized himself. *Is that me?* he asked himself. *Is that the man who is going to help the world?*

He was only vaguely aware of the figure that appeared at his shoulder. Then there was a light touch on his arm. "You look so lonely, sitting here all by yourself," a voice said.

He blinked. It was Jessica Hopkins standing beside him—smiling, a warmth in her eyes.

"It's good to see you," he said, inadequately.

"Why don't you join us?"

"Us?" He turned, saw Harold Stern sitting in a booth.

"The end of the day," she said. "Would you rather be alone? I don't want to intrude on your—"

"Of course not," he said.

He picked up his drink and followed her over to the booth, watching the way she walked. It was hard, Regan thought, for a woman to seem beautiful from the rear, but Jessica did. Her rust-colored knit suit clung to her tightly, making Regan think how good it would be to hold her, follow those soft curves with his hands. He remembered that night when he had wanted her. What would have happened then, if Grace had not come out?

Harold Stern was a small, muscular man in his early thirties—balding, spectacled. He rose as they approached and held out his hand to Regan. "It's been a long time, Paul."

"Too long," Regan answered, shaking hands, feeling the strength in the other man's grip. Stern, he recalled, had been an All-American at some midwestern university. "How goes the battle?"

"Lousy, as usual. And you?"

Regan sat down beside Jessica, opposite Stern. He noted the way Stern's eyes followed Jessica when she moved. There was desire there, desire and love.

Regan sipped at his drink. "I imagine we all have our ups and downs."

"A very profound statement," Stern said dryly.

"Harold, please," said Jessica. She turned sideways, facing Regan. "Harold isn't his usual self."

"You don't need to apologize for me," Stern said. Then he smiled suddenly. The smile did something to his face, made it younger, much less severe.

"It has been a horrible day," Stern said. "One of those days. Sometimes—well, sometimes I get the feeling that the whole damned thing is just so much waste of time. We try to help, Paul. We try so damned hard. Perhaps too hard."

"Let's talk about something more pleasant," Jessica suggested.

"What in hell could be pleasant tonight?" Stern grumbled.

"Oh, Harold!" She was suddenly angry.

"Perhaps you two would rather be alone," Regan said.

"No, not that," Stern said. "I'm just in a bitch of a mood, Paul. Sorry." He took out a cigarette, lit it. "I shouldn't be with other people when I feel like this. I should be alone. Do you believe in getting drunk, good and drunk?" He was staring intently at Paul.

Paul grinned. "Sometimes that's the only answer. A damned good drunk."

"Let's get drunk," Stern said.

"A good idea. I feel like getting drunk."

"We'll all three get drunk and then we'll all three go up to Jessica's. What do you think of that?"

"I think it's a wonderful idea."

"And we'll both sleep with Jessica."

"Wonderful."

"Stop it! Both of you." Jessica was smiling, not quite sure whether or not the two men were kidding. "My love life is my own affair."

"You need loving, Jessie," Stern said grimly.

"What I need is my own business."

Regan motioned for more drinks. He was slumped against the back of the booth, only half listening. Here they were, three intelligent people, three responsible people in the community, talking like a trio of guttersnipes. It could lead to no good. He looked at Jessica. It had been almost two weeks since he had slept with Grace. He had thought that he could never feel anything again, not after the violence of their passion, the sustained, night-after-night

128

sexual bouts, and now he was thinking about this woman beside him.

"The good doctor," Stern said, "is getting ideas. He is looking at your breasts, my dear, sizing them up, wondering about them."

"Damn you, Harold!" she snapped. "Keep your mind out of the gutter for a little while at least."

"I deal with the gutter," he replied.

"I'm sure," Regan said, measuring his words, "there must be some other topic of conversation we could discuss."

"Sure there is. How about your wife? I hear a lot about her these days."

Regan looked quietly across the table at Stern, suddenly hating the man, deeply and intensely. He put his hands flat on the table and leaned forward.

"How would you like to step outside? How would you like to go outside with me and let me beat the living hell out of you?"

Stern said, "Screw you, buddy!"

Paul made a move to get out of the booth, but Jessica's hand restrained him. "No, Paul. Please. Don't do anything like that."

Stern was already standing. He looked down at them and then, suddenly, threw back his head and laughed. "I'll be damned," he said. "I'll be holy damned, Paul. I must be acting like a real nut." He leaned down, put a hand on Paul's shoulder. "I'm taking everything out on you. Forgive me. I didn't mean that about your wife. Forget it."

"It's forgotten."

"Look—" he stood upright again, waving his hands helplessly—"I'm all balled up inside. I apologize for

129

the way I've been acting. Like I said, I shouldn't be with other people when I feel like this. I'm going on home and go to bed with a bottle and feel sorry for myself. I'll wake up tomorrow with the damnedest hangover ever, but I'll feel better for it.

"You two sit here, be nice to each other. You're both nice people, believe me. I just—oh hell, I'll just go along. See her home for me, will you, Paul?"

The next moment he was gone.

"Please don't think badly of him, Paul," Jessica said.

"I don't."

"This job—what he's trying to do is too much. No man can take on what he has, and still be normal twenty-four hours a day." She put her hand over his, squeezing lightly. "I'm sorry. I suppose you're a lot like Harold, too. Both of you, trying to do so much more than you can."

"You're feeling sorry for everyone tonight."

"I guess I am."

She took her hand away from his and began playing with the stem of her glass, staring down at it idly, lost in thought. "I wish—" she said, and stopped.

"What?"

"I wish we had met some other way. I've thought so often how silly I must have seemed that day I came to your office."

"You weren't silly."

"But I was. I know I was. Paul?"

"What?"

"I don't want to be alone tonight. I don't want to sit here."

"And?"

"I don't want you to misunderstand me. Please don't. But let's leave here. Let's go to my place and I'll fix something to eat and we'll just sit around and talk."

"Is that all?"

"That's all it can be."

She laughed, nervously. "Damn," she said, "it almost sounds as if I'm propositioning you. I don't mean it that way. I know you're married. I know—"

"You know many things. I accept your invitation."

"With no strings attached?"

"With no strings attached."

"Paul, you're a nice guy."

She had said that once before, somewhere. Hadn't she? Had that been in this lifetime? His head was fuzzy, and he knew it was not from the drinks.

"I'm a wonderful guy," he said. "I have a great big shoulder and you can cry on it all you want to."

"You need to cry, too."

He looked at her carefully, and he saw that she meant what she said. She returned his steady gaze, unblinkingly.

131

14

JESSICA had a small, one-bedroom house, a few blocks from the beach. It was warm and cozy inside, and furnished in a neat, feminine, unostentatious manner. One wall of the living room was completely filled with bookshelves.

She left him for a minute. When he was alone, he saw the painting he had given her—the one Grace had wanted to burn. He could not understand how he had missed it when he first entered. It was prominently displayed on the wall opposite the bookshelves.

He stood filling his pipe, staring up at the painting —struck again by the simple beauty of it. The artist had captured a mood of tranquility and peace. Regan hadn't realized how much he had missed the painting. He remembered how happy he had been when Grace had given it to him. "This is the way our marriage will be, darling," she had said. "This is what I want for our marriage." She had smiled, disarmingly. "At least, in the daytime."

Jessica said, behind him, "It is beautiful. I often sit

here at night and look up at it. It gives me a—I don't know how to explain it. I can feel all mixed up inside, horribly depressed after something has gone wrong, and I sit and look at it and things just seem to get better."

He turned. She was holding a tray with bottles of gin and vermouth, glasses, a pitcher, a bowl of ice cubes. The top of her head just reached the point of his chin and as he looked down at her, she moved her eyes away from him, those bluish-green eyes that seemed to take in so much.

"Don't be afraid of me, Jessica," he said.

"What a horribly silly thing to say." She tried to smile. She moved away, putting the tray on a coffee table.

"Is it so silly?"

"Please, Paul. Remember what we said?"

"What did we say?"

"Just—nothing. Just a quiet dinner."

He nodded slowly.

"You should kick me out the door, Jessica. I'm standing here, looking at you, thinking evil thoughts. What Harold said in the bar was true. I was looking at your breasts, wondering—no, never mind. I am guilty. I throw myself on your mercy. I am also guilty of trying to analyze you and I shouldn't do that."

She smiled back at him. "You admit your guilt and I sentence you to one Jessica Hopkins dinner—a horrible fate, worse than death. You mix the drinks and I'll be back in ten minutes."

Regan busied himself with mixing the martinis, wondering if he should call Grace and tell her he would be late. But what good would that do?

When Jessica returned, he handed her a martini and they sat on the couch.

"I'll never forget you for that night," he said. "You were the one redeeming pleasure in an otherwise insane evening."

"You're talking about the night at the Club?"

"I don't know what I would have done if you hadn't been there. It made me feel better just to see you standing there."

"You're very complimentary tonight. Is this your usual style?"

"I have no idea." He leaned back, contented, sipping at his martini. "I am as I am."

"A rose is a rose is a rose?"

"Something like that."

She bent across the coffee table, took a cigarette from a ceramic box. Her breasts moved excitingly as she did so, and his eyes lingered on them.

"If," he said quietly, "you want to keep my mind from wandering to other things, you should bind yourself tightly." She blushed, sitting up. "There's nothing that can be done about that. I'm—wearing a brassiere. You will just have to show more strength of character."

"You don't mind if I have my own personal thoughts, do you?"

"Of course not."

He finished his martini, poured himself another. He noticed that Jessica was wearing the same charm bracelet she had worn in his office. He tried to recall whether or not she had been wearing it that night at the Club. It was out of key with the rest of her. It was the kind of thing a teen-ager would wear—

134

dime-store jewelry. He played a mental game with himself, trying to imagine who had given her the bracelet—a wartime lover, killed later? No, she was too young for that.

Jessica finished her own martini. He poured her another one while she put some records on the hi-fi. The rich strains of a Chopin waltz filled the room. Watching Jessica cross the room again, Regan had an almost overpowering impulse to grab at her, pull her to him.

"The wench is very provocative," he said.

"The male is preoccupied with sex," she replied.

"Aren't we all?"

"You sound like—" She did not go on.

"Like who? Harold?"

"As a matter of fact, yes."

"Is that so bad? The poor man desires you. This poor man does the same. You are shaped to be desired. You're dressed for the same." He rose. "Come here, wench."

"No."

He reached out for her and she danced away from him, laughing. He was making a fool of himself, perhaps, but the desire in him was too strong to be denied. She skipped farther away, still laughing, her red mouth wantonly open. He caught her by the arm, pulled her to him, locked his body against hers, felt her own desire in the warmth and trembling of her flesh. Their mouths met, locked silently, opened so that their tongues could meet. She was moaning, pushing herself against him, grinding her body against him—and he swept one arm down behind her knees, lifted her off her feet, and put her down gently on the couch.

He was over her, looking down into her face. He saw tears trickling from the corners of her closed eyes. Her mouth was working. Her body writhed in an agony of need—and then her eyes opened as he started down on top of her and she screamed, "No! Please, no!" The anguish of her scream, the horrible fear in it, caught and held him.

She turned her head away, forcing it into the back of the couch to muffle her sobs. He put a hand tentatively on her hair, stroked it. He was shaking with the want of her, but he fought against himself and won.

He moved away, stood in the middle of the room, trying to calm his racing heart. He stared at the painting on the wall—kept staring at it. Slowly his desire subsided.

After a long time Jessica turned on the couch, sat up, smoothed out her clothing. She ran the backs of her hands across her eyes, wiping away the tears.

"I'm sorry, Paul."

"Forget it." There was a hint of anger in his voice, and he immediately felt sorry for it.

"I just—can't go through with it."

"Don't explain it to me. Don't do that."

She tried smiling; it was only half successful. "You're angry with me now, and I don't blame you."

"Don't be so critical of yourself."

She bent her head. "One more martini," she said, "and then I think dinner will be ready. I—feel the need of a drink at this moment."

"You mean you want me to stay?"

"Very much."

Regan was baffled. It was not reasonable for her to refuse him and yet want him to stay. But since when had there been any logic in the relations of men and women? He was asking too much. She was beautiful and desirable, but she had turned him down—it was that simple.

Well, why not stay?

They had finished the simple dinner. Now Regan sat back, smoking, relaxed.

"Paul?" Jessica was curled up on the couch, feet tucked under her, one arm stretched out along the back of the couch. "Can you tell me something?"

"I'll try."

"Why were you going to destroy that painting?"

Regan hesitated. "No good reason," he said. "I just got tired of it."

"I'd rather you just told me it was none of my business."

"All right. It's none of your business."

"I'll accept that." She paused a moment, as if she wanted to bring up another subject, but could not quite bring herself to do it. Finally she said, "I imagine it's hard for you, being with people like me, just people."

"Why should it be hard?"

"Everyone is wary around you. They're afraid of making some Freudian slip of the tongue, afraid of what you might think." She grinned, almost happily. "I'm deathly afraid of what you think of me after— after the way I—put you off."

"That's a polite way of saying it. However, there's

137

no reason you should be afraid of what I think. My opinion of you has not changed. I still think you're an intelligent, beautiful woman. I had ideas that I would like to do the obvious with you. Simple. You said no. Again, simple."

"Can I talk to you? I mean as a friend, not as a psychiatrist?"

"It's sometimes difficult to differentiate between the two, but go ahead and try me."

"I will." She sighed deeply. She held up her wrist, dangling the charm bracelet. "This—this was given to me a long time ago, Paul, almost ten years ago. I had a silly, schoolgirl crush on my English teacher in high school. You know the kind of thing. Only with me, well, it was different.

"The teacher had a crush on me, too. He really loved me. He had a room in a boarding house, and I'd sneak in there at dark and we'd lie on his bed and talk and dream together. He had the softest hands, almost like velvet." She raised her own hands, stared at them. "Anyway—" and she sounded suddenly like a little girl—"anyway, nothing ever happened. We would lie there and he would undress me and pet me all over, stroke me the way some people stroke a cat. He'd kiss my breasts and recite poetry to me and stroke me. And Paul, this is the honest truth, we never went all the way. I wanted to. God! how I wanted to. It went on for almost six months, night after night, and we would play together, like a couple of kids not knowing what they were doing. But he would never do it to me, never, not even when I begged him to. He would say that I was too clean, that I shouldn't dirty myself that way.

"God, Paul, it was pure hell. Honestly."

He emptied his pipe out into an ashtray. "Do you mean to tell me that you and this man shared a bed like that for six months and—nothing happened?"

"That's what I'm saying."

He tried unsuccessfully to hold back his laughter. "I'm sorry, Jessica. But I'm not laughing at you. The whole thing is so damned ridiculous. Was he a homosexual?"

"I don't think so. I loved him, deeply and intensely. He gave me this—" she held up the wrist with the charm bracelet again—"the last night we were together. After that, he just disappeared. I never knew what happened to him. He left school. To this day, I don't know where he is or what happened to him."

"And you still wear that bracelet?"

"Yes."

"Why?"

She hesitated. "I'm not sure."

Regan stretched out his legs, cupped his hands behind his head. He felt sorry for Jessica. He could imagine the torment she had gone through—young girl, hopelessly in love with an older, supposedly intelligent man.

"What do you want from me?" he asked. "Do you want me to tell you why you still wear the bracelet? Is that it?"

"I don't want you to tell me anything. It's a story I've never told anyone, not even—"

"Not even Harold Stern?"

"That's right. Is it that obvious, the way I feel about him?"

139

"I was thinking it was the other way around, the way he felt about you."

"He—he says he loves me. He wants me—the way you wanted me before."

He leaned forward, resting his elbows on his knees. "Jessica, there's nothing wrong in sex, as such. There's nothing to hide. You are a mature woman, a very desirable woman. I'm not advising you to go ahead and have an affair with Harold Stern or with anyone else, but if you repress your emotions, then the consequences are often much worse."

"That's easy for a man to say."

"What are you trying to protect? Harold is certainly intelligent enough to realize that, at your age, you're no longer a virgin. Is that what you're afraid of, what he'll think? Give the man a little credit, Jessica. In this day and age, it's a virtual impossibility for a woman to reach twenty-five and still be a virgin. Don't think badly of yourself."

"You don't understand."

"Maybe not. I gave you my own viewpoint."

"But that's exactly it, you're missing the whole point."

She put her feet on the floor, leaning forward, in the same position as his, elbows on knees. Their faces were only inches apart.

"You see, Paul," she said, looking directly into his eyes. "I lied to him. I got caught in my own little lie. I told him that—that I wasn't a virgin, and now he can't understand why I won't go to bed with him. Silly, isn't it?"

"You mean—"

"I mean that I am a virgin, a frightened virgin."

140

Regan recovered slowly from his surprise. "How foolish you are, Jessica," he said gently. He raised one hand, ran it along her cheek. "How very foolish."

"Kiss me."

Their mouths met. Slowly and sensuously, they kissed, while their bodies were still apart. Then they were together, arms locked around each other, while they fell endlessly into a fit of desire.

15

LOOKING AT GRACE as she stood in front of the fireplace, Regan hardly recognized her. She was smoking
a cigarette in quick, nervous drags. She looked worn,
almost haggard. Her hair was lifeless, her movements
sluggish. Her pale pink skirt was soiled; the darker
pink pullover had a hole in one sleeve.

"I'm very tired, Paul," she said.

"You know what I've said all along. You must see
Dr. Werner. You can't go on like this, Grace."

"Where were you last night?"

"What difference does it make? This is no home
for me any more. You know something, Grace—I
dread coming here every night. I can't go on this way
with you. I've—just about had it."

"Then why don't you run to Jessica Hopkins? I'm
sure she'll welcome you."

Regan was stunned. How could she know about
Jessica?

"Don't look so shocked, Paul, I know all about you.
I know where you were last night. I only wanted you

142

to tell me. I thought perhaps you would. I thought—"
She shook her head.

"Grace," he said, "just this once, you tell me something. Who told you about those conversations with my patients? How did you know I was with Jessica last night?"

She laughed harshly. "How stupid do you think I am? I'm going to ruin you, Paul, and I'm going to ruin Jessica Hopkins, too. To hell with you both!"

Regan walked out. He got into the car and drove aimlessly, trying not to think. After a long time, he found himself on Jessica's street.

He had no conscious recollection of deciding to come here. Was it an accident—or something more?

With sudden decision, he parked at the curb, got out and rang Jessica's bell.

Jessica came to the door almost immediately, dressed in a loose-fitting sweater and shorts. To Regan's surprise, she did not seem at all embarrassed to see him. "Ah, the great lover," she said with a happy smile, and motioned him in.

Feeling oddly guilty, Regan followed her into the house.

She faced him. "Have you come to swear undying devotion? Or to tell me that you want to make an honest woman of me?"

Regan looked at her without answering, trying to make sure there was no bitterness under her light manner.

"Paul, please don't look so glum. The world is not coming to an end. In fact, I woke up this morning feeling like a new woman." She laughed. "I guess I am a new woman. I'm no longer a little girl, hiding

143

her emotions behind a childish symbol. See?" She lifted her wrist and he saw that the charm bracelet was gone. "I threw it away, thanks to you. Paul, you're marvelous.

"Jessica, I—"

"Don't say it, Paul. Don't say anything. It just happened, that's all, and I'm happy because of it. I know you don't love me and I don't love you. I love Harold and you love your wife—it was just something that happened between us. It had to happen, eventually, and I'm glad it was you."

Regan felt immeasurably relieved and tried to tell her so.

She interrupted him gently. "I'm glad you came for another reason," she said. "I have—something for you. Paul, this is about your trouble with your wife. Maybe—just maybe—this will explain a little of it. It's sort of scary. Wait here." She went into the bedroom and came back in a moment carrying a spool of tape. She fitted the spool onto the tape deck of the hi-fi, turned on the machine.

"Don't ask any questions yet. Just sit there and listen."

He did as he was told. In a moment, he heard his own voice and the voice of Jeanne Higgins. He recognized what they were saying—it was the tape of their session the week before last. But someone had edited the tape so that instead of doctor and patient, they sounded like lovers. Listening to it was more than Regan could take.

"Stop it!" he said.

She turned off the machine. "This came by special messenger this morning, Paul. I don't know who sent it, or why it was sent to me. But whoever did this is obviously trying to ruin you."

Regan thought he could guess. Grace, in the sickness of her mind, could be trying to destroy him this way. She might have sent this tape to Jessica, hoping to turn her against him.

He felt nauseated. His whole world, the world he had built for himself so carefully, had come down in ruins.

He got up and went to the door. His legs felt stiff and heavy.

"Don't give up, Paul," Jessica said, in a low voice. "You're too strong to give up. Just remember."

"Remember what?"

"Remember what I was before you came along. I'm a woman now, Paul. I thank you for that—I love you for it." She smiled. "Now go and be strong, and find your own happiness."

16

Be strong, she had said, and find your own happiness.

He had believed in Grace, loved her, and now she was trying to ruin him. It would be simple for her to get into his office, to get copies of his tapes of sessions. That was how she had managed to memorize all those conversations. He could picture her, sitting alone, listening to the tapes over and over, perverting them in her own mind, condemning him.

A black-and-white police car was parked in front of his house, its red light blinking on and off. Regan's dull senses quickened. What could Grace have done now?

Grace was in the living room, huddled up on the couch, her face in her hands, shoulders jerking. A big, red-faced man stood up as Paul entered. "Dr. Regan?"

"That's right."

"I'd like to talk to you alone, doctor."

146

They went into the next room. "I'm Detective-Sergeant Quinn, Dr. Regan. We got a call from your wife, saying she was going to kill herself. I rush like hell getting over here, and now she denies making the call. Now I ask you, who in hell would call and say somebody else was going to commit suicide? It don't make sense to me. Maybe it does to you. You're one of them doctors, aren't you?"

"Yes." Regan was puzzled. He could not believe that Grace would actually attempt suicide. "Just leave it to me, Sergeant. I'll handle it."

He let Quinn out. When he came back into the living room Grace was gone.

A shock of fright went through him as he heard a noise from the kitchen. He ran into the kitchen, stopped abruptly when he saw Grace standing at the counter, calmly measuring coffee into the electric coffee-maker. She looked at him with surprise.

"Are you actually that worried about me, Paul?"

He raised his hands. "Right at this moment, Grace, I'm not sure of anything. I've never been so completely confused and befuddled in my life."

"Darling—no." She shook her head. "I have no right to call you that, not now, not after—what I've put you through these past few months. Paul, I'm—terribly sorry."

"That doesn't help much."

"No, I guess it doesn't. It's only that—Oh, hell."

"Grace, what am I supposed to think? That man said you called the police, told them you were going to kill yourself."

"Do you believe that?"

147

"It isn't unlikely. Contrary to popular belief, people who threaten to commit suicide often do so."

"That's Dr. Regan, the learned psychiatrist, speaking. I want to hear what my husband thinks."

"All right. No, I don't believe it. I can't explain why. God knows you've done enough crazy things in the last few months. But I don't think you could do that."

She came towards him, slowly, tentatively. She stopped, looking intently into his face, and he could see she was near tears again.

"Paul, Paul," she whispered, coming into his arms.

He held her close and said nothing.

They stood that way for a while, the moments ticked by, and suddenly Regan knew that would be all right. Despite everything that had happened, it would be all right.

She pulled her head back, looking up into his face. "Kiss me, Paul. Gently, very gently."

His lips met hers.

When the kiss ended, she pushed him away. Her shoulders were firmer now; she seemed to be standing up straighter. "Let's have some coffee while I bare my soul," she said.

They sat at the kitchen table, drinking coffee. Regan filled his pipe.

Grace was subdued.

"Don't say anything for a while, darling," she began. "Please don't. Just let me talk. Just let me tell you." She studied her hands, folded quietly on the top of the table.

"Paul, for months I've been receiving tapes of your sessions. They've all been delivered by special messenger. I'm sorry, Paul. They just kept coming and I wasn't strong enough not to listen to them.

"I couldn't help myself. I'd sit here, all alone, listening to those tapes, listening to your voice and the voices of those women, and I would go almost out of my mind. I wanted to kill them—I wanted to kill you. I wanted—oh, hell, what difference does it make? It's done now. I suppose I've ruined what was between us."

She looked into his eyes. "Paul, tonight, this call made me realize something. I know now that someone is trying to destroy us."

Regan sat motionless for a long moment. He thought he understood the whole situation now. It seemed very simple, and he wondered that he had not seen it long before.

He rose, and went around the table. He put a hand under Grace's chin.

"Trust me, Grace. I think I know the answer. I'll be back as soon as I can."

"I trust you."

Before he left the house, Regan put in a call to Dr. Werner, asking him to meet him at a certain address.

There was surprise on Sara's face when she opened the door—surprise and shock.

"May I come in, Sara?"

She blinked rapidly, looking out into the hallway as if she expected someone to be with him.

"Well, Sara?"

"I—I'm alone, Dr. Regan. I don't think—it wouldn't be right. Your wife might not understand."

"I'm sure she wouldn't mind."

"Well—"

"I want to talk to you, Sara."

She licked her lips, still confused. One hand played with the doorknob, the other came up to her throat.

Regan pushed by her, into the room. Then he stopped abruptly.

The room was small and crowded. One whole wall was covered with photographs of Regan. He could not guess how Sara had managed to get so many. He saw the pipe rack on a table beside the couch—recognized two of his own pipes that he had thought were lost. An old sweater of his was hanging over a chair.

He turned slowly, looking at Sara. She had closed the door, was leaning against it, eyes closed.

"All right," she said, "so I'm a thief. So I took a few of your things."

"You're more than a thief, Sara."

"Yes. Of course."

She opened her eyes, took a step towards him. "I'm much more than a thief, Dr. Regan. Much, much more. I'm a woman.

"I've wanted you, oh, so much. How I've wanted you! I've wanted to hold your face in my hands, feel your lips against mine, press my body against yours.

"You're too good for them. You don't belong to them. Not to your wife or any of the others. She has you at night, damn her soul to hell! You think I don't know about it. I lie here every night, in my lonely bed, thinking of what you're doing with her, and I want you for myself. You belong to me, do you understand that? You belong to me!"

150

"Sara—"

"No! I can't take it any longer! It was bad enough when you were having her, sleeping with her every night. But you had to go to that other one, that Jessica Hopkins. I couldn't stand that. One was enough. You know something? That day in the office, that day with Jeanne—I wanted you to rip my clothes off. I wanted you to hurt me. I wanted you to take me and love me. I wanted, oh, my darling love, I wanted—so much." Her voice had sunk to a whisper. She dropped to the floor, kneeling as if in prayer, eyes closed, hands clasped together.

Regan tried to feel sorry for her, and failed. She was pitiful, a lost soul, and yet he could only stand there and damn her, damn her for everything that had happened to him, damn her for almost ruining him and the woman he loved.

"Sara, you sent those tapes to Grace."

"Yes."

"And you called the police."

"Yes."

"Did you follow me to Jessica's—call Grace about that?"

"What else could I do?"

She opened her eyes. "You don't know what love is," she screamed. "But I do! I do! I love you! You're mine!"

Regan stooped down, picked her up. Momentarily she fought against him, then she was quiet in his arms. He put her gently on the couch. She stared up at him unseeingly. She was a long way off, somewhere in her own world.

Dr. Werner arrived a little later. Paul left Sara

with him, knowing the long struggle she was going to have, knowing how difficult it would be for her. In a way, he felt sorry for her.

But he could not forgive her, and he knew he never would.

17

THE NIGHT was still. Regan lay with his hands cupped behind his head. Grace stirred sleepily, murmured something he could not hear, and moved against him.

"It's all right now, my darling," he whispered, putting an arm around her, holding her close.

"Darling."

"I thought you were asleep."

"I was."

"It's—good to be back, Grace."

"It's wonderful, darling. Please, let's never—go through anything like that again."

He kissed her hair. "I feel sorry for her," she said. "Very sorry. She has no one and I have you. That's all I want."

"You'll need time, Grace."

"I know."

"Maybe we could go away. Mexico City. We'll take a long vacation, just the two of us."

"No."

"What?"

"I said no."

"Why not? I think—"

Her fingers covered his lips. "Be quiet. Don't talk, my darling. We don't need to run away; we don't need that. You can help me and I'll help myself. You can't leave your patients. It would be unfair to you. You have responsibilities and I will not let you throw them away.

"And even if the women are all wrapped up in you sexually, even if they do tell you all those things—I'll have you every night, and that's all I want."

She rolled over onto him, and they were both laughing.

"Love me," she murmured.

"Again?"

"Again and again and again, my darling."

END

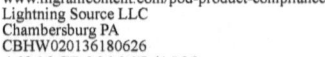